The Lady With The Laptop

CLIVE SINCLAIR is the author of four novels and two collections of short stories, including the prize-winning *Hearts of Gold*. In 1981 he was awarded a Bicentennial Arts Fellowship and in 1983 was chosen as one of the twenty Best of Young British Novelists. In 1988 he was the British Council Guest Writer in Residence at the University of Uppsala, Sweden. More recently he has been the British Library Penguin Writer's Fellow. He has a doctorate from the University of East Anglia, and is a fellow of the Royal Society of Literature. Clive Sinclair lives in St Albans with his teenage son.

CLIVE SINCLAIR

The Lady With The Laptop

and other stories

PICADOR

First published 1996 by Picador

This edition published 1997 by Picador
an imprint of Macmillan Publishers Ltd
25 Eccleston Place, London SW1W 9NF
and Basingstoke

Associated companies throughout the world

ISBN 0 330 34840 X

1 3 5 7 9 8 6 4 2

A CIP catalogue record for this book is available from
the British Library.

Typeset by CentraCet, Cambridge
Printed and bound in Great Britain by
Mackays of Chatham plc, Chatham, Kent

Contents

IN MEMORY OF FRAN (1947–1994)

ACKNOWLEDGEMENTS

Early versions of 'Las Fiestas de Navidad' and 'My CV' first appeared in the *Guardian* and the *Jewish Chronicle* (Literary Supplement). An even earlier version of 'The Iceman Cometh' was published (in Serbo-Croat) in the magazine *Mezuza* (a non-sectarian anachronism in Belgrade). 'The Lady With The Laptop' appeared as is in *Granta 51*. Thanks are due to Matthew Fort, Gerald Jacobs, David Albahari, and Ian Jack. The author also wishes to put on record his gratitude to The Royal Literary Fund, Yosl & Audrey Bergner, Pamela & Jonathan Lubell, Sarah Spankie, Ivor Abrahams, David & Seth Sinclair.

'The lines are fallen unto me in pleasant places . . .'
Psalm xvi

· PART I ·

Las Fiestas de Navidad

MOTHER OF GOD, my teeth! They ache like a guilty conscience. Forgive me, my molars, for all the *gringas rubias* – those sugary skulls with the features of foreign blondes – I have devoured since the Day of the Dead, since *Todos Santos*. But tell me, my teeth, how could I resist *la muerte sexy*, as they call those tempting candies in that *dulceria* near Toluca? Soon I must go to my brother-in-law, the dentist, and pay for my sins, pray for an *extraccíon sin dolor*. In the meantime I must bear the pain and greet the happy couple who have come to Mexico to make their own *extraccíon sin dolor*. That is why I am standing in the middle of the airport with my little flag. I am a guide. As footnotes are to texts, so am I to my country; a moveable asterisk. My task is to amuse and instruct the two Anglos whilst they await their ersatz *navidad*, and then to assist them as they painlessly extract the newborn from his homeland.

Being well read in contemporary fiction you will doubtless be familiar with the concept of *magical realism*, but how many of you have heard of the *probability mechanism*? It is the invention of the *Secretaria de Hacienda y Credito Publico*, more familiarly known as the Customs and Excise. Having collected their baggage all new arrivals must push a random selection button. If a green light appears the traveller is permitted to proceed without any inspection. A red light is a different matter.

Unlucky Rosie and Rupert are subjected to a prolonged search and interrogation before being finally admitted. Both have flushed cheeks by the time they find me. 'This is a bloody country!' says Rupert. He does not know how bloody! The probability mechanism is actually a variant upon an experiment first tried in the beautiful city of Guanajuato more than a century ago. There was a revolt. The Spaniards retaliated with the so-called *lottery of death*. Simple rules. The names of all the citizens were collected, after which there was a draw. The winners were first tortured, then executed. Some things improve, even in the Third World. Nowadays they are merely questioned.

Rupert, however, remains the epitome of ingratitude. To quell his agitation he withdraws a packet of chewing gum from his pocket. Remembering his manners he offers me a piece. 'You'll like this,' he says. 'It's a new line from Rigoletto, called Decadent.'

'It's Rupert's baby,' says Rosie proudly. 'He's a copywriter. He invented the name.'

Invented the name? *Señora*, we invented the product. Originally known as *chicle*, it is the coagulated juice of the indigenous sapodilla tree. If it weren't for the Mexicans, *señora*, the Anglo-Saxons would still be masticating paraffin wax, and Rigoletto would not be a multinational conglomerate. 'Look,' says Rupert, unurapping a stick, 'black chewing gum. Very *fin de siècle*, don't you think?'

Everyone has a conspiracy theory. Some people blame the Zionists for all the world's ills. Others cite terrorists. I accuse Rigoletto. They have a motive. Any encyclopaedia will inform you that the use of chewing gum rises in periods of social tension. In my opinion we are all but the playthings of gum-toting capitalists.

'What flavour is it?' I ask.

'Peppermint,' he replies.

'*Por favor, señor*,' I exclaim, shaking my head, 'do you not know that peppermint reduces a man's potency?' The blood suddenly departs from Rupert's cheeks. Oh, I am a wicked man! I could no more resist taunting Rupert than I could shun the *dulces* that have rotted my teeth. You see, my friends, I happen to know that his sperm count is even lower than my annual income. That is why they are here. Rosie gives the green light, but poor Rupert's tadpoles can't even make first base.

They have reservations at the Hotel Majestic on Constitution Square, which we locals call the *zócalo*. Jaime, the handsome lawyer, is already there, slumped like an invertebrate in a leather armchair. He rises as we approach and embraces his clients. 'It is good to feel the flesh,' he says, as I complete the formalities at the reception desk, 'the fax is efficient, but it transmits no flavours. In Mexico, as you will discover, we thrive upon sensation.' As if to demonstrate the accuracy of this statement he leads us to the famous restaurant on the seventh floor, where a fat waiter in a short red coat seats us *al fresco* although, it must be said, the air is hardly fresh.

'Once the white peaks of Popocatepetl and Ixtacchihuatl could be seen from here on clear days,' I say. 'Alas, no longer. Constitution Square is clearly visible, however. Look around and you will see a panorama of our history. Tucked away in the north-eastern corner are the relics of the Aztec Templo Mayor, where old Mr Chacmool reclines with his empty plate always asking for more; more hearts, more viscera. Don't look so worried, my friends; neither is on the menu today. The temple was only rediscovered in 1978 when workers accidentally unearthed a stone which, scholars say, shows how Coatlicue became pregnant whilst sweeping its floor. Perhaps you should follow her example, *señora*. Who knows what may happen?' Rupert is not amused. 'That other divinely impregnated virgin is honoured next door,' I continue, 'in the basilicas and baroque churches built by Cortés and his devout successors.' Finally, I indicate the eighteenth-century building that fills the entire east side of the great plaza. 'Behold the Presidential Palace,' I say, 'within which our entire history is retold yet again in Diego Rivera's flamboyant murals.'

'What a fascinating place,' says Rosie politely.

Then *la comida* begins. Despite all Jaime's eloquent advertisements for the specialities of the house the English insist upon plain *biftec de res* which they wash down with bottles of Sol. I drink plenty of tequila to anaesthetize my aching gums. 'Everything is progressing beautifully,' says Jaime to the expectant couple. 'The mother has already felt the first pains of labour, the judge is already inking the rubber stamp.' He raises his glass. 'Today is the first of December,' he announces, 'I have no doubt that you will be

4

celebrating *las fiestas de navidad* in London with your new baby.'

After lunch Rosie retires to enjoy a siesta. Jaime returns to his office or his mistress. I enter the *zócalo* with Rupert. Around its perimeter are numerous shoe-shiners, whose purpose is to serve businessmen as they stream towards their various avenues. Of course they are contemptuous of my shop-soiled sneakers, but are prepared to kill for the honour of polishing Rupert's boots, fresh from the shelves of some fine emporium in his capital's ritziest quarter.

One shoe-shine boy catches my eye. Like the other menials he is squatting at the feet of an enthroned executive. But in this case the proper connection does not seem to have been made. While the latter is leafing through *La Prensa* (headline: ALTA AL SMOG), the former is deep into a sleazy comic-book entitled *Sensacional de Barrios*. Suddenly the faces change. The world has become a mirror. I am the lazy half-wit lost in a dream of bright colours and cheap thrills, while Rupert sits on his lofty perch and ponders the real world's problems. Only with difficulty do I cast off the vision, blaming it on the tequila and the poor visibility.

The *zócalo* is like an aquarium teeming with life. Women squat in front of the cathedral surrounded by their wares and their offspring. Babies are everywhere, staggering on unsteady pins or tightly wrapped in their mother's *rebozo*. Such an abundance of vitality naturally attracts predators. Some of these children will undoubtedly die. So who can blame their mothers if they give them to foreigners? And who can blame the childless strangers who take them? We follow the beat of bone flutes and drums and find born-again Aztecs in loincloths and feather headdresses dancing outside the Templo Mayor. A crowd gathers. Only my companion remains unmoved.

Days pass and, despite my best efforts, Rosie and Rupert refuse to amend their prejudices. They will not touch our food, nor visit our museums. Trotsky's house in Coyoacán is dismissed as a symbol of a system that has been universally discredited. They are clearly repelled by the peasants at Guadalope, who enter the cathedral on bleeding knees and ask for the impossible. 'I feel my cynicism is misplaced,' says Rupert, as he watches the slow progress across the plaza. I feel like telling him to pray for an increase in his sperm count.

Even the ruins of Teotihuacán fail to impress them. Rupert's pompous response puts me in mind of an even more contemptuous predecesssor, a minor Egyptian playwright I had the misfortune to escort a few seasons ago. His name escapes me; rhymes with Conan the Barbarian, Yonnan something-or-other. Anyway, he stepped out of the van, took one look at the magnificent site and turned to his wife (who was grumpily attending to their babies). 'You're not missing much,' he reported, 'these are not real pyramids at all, merely platforms with an over-active thyroid.' He looked at me accusingly. 'The originals in Giza – *our* pyramids – are proper buildings with complex interiors.' According to Rupert they are 'nice'. When pressed he is prepared to admit that they are 'attractive and quite interesting'. He has his reward. Jaime ceases to come to the hotel in person. He merely sends a daily fax which says, in effect, *manana*.

By 22 December Rosie is desperate. We are in a tourist restaurant in the *zona rosa*. '*Tiene huevos?*' she enquires, when the waiter appears. 'OK,' she snaps, as he takes our order to the kitchen, 'tell me why he was smirking.'

'You thought you were saying, "Do you have eggs?"' I explain, 'but in fact you were asking the waiter whether he had balls.'

Rosie does not see the joke. 'I've had enough!' she cries. 'I'm homesick. Literally. I swear I'll puke if I see another bloody *tamale*. Don't you understand? I want a proper Christmas dinner.'

'My wife is a bit of a blue-blood,' explains Rupert, 'she values her traditions.' *Her* traditions! *Señora* you are like all the English; nothing but a plagiarist who, having made your forgery, denigrates the original.

When Montezuma dined hunchbacks and dwarves entertained him with jokes and dancing. What amuses you in England, *señora*? You pull crackers. You wear paper crowns. You tell one another foolish jokes. Is this what you miss? Or is it the food? Your tasteless roast turkey is but the last faint echo of the lordly *mole poblano de guajolote* which Montezuma ate off red and black Cholula ware. Lady, you have undoubtedly forgotten that it was his people – *my* people – who first domesticated the *guajolote* or turkey. *Your* traditions? No Englishman saw a turkey before 1540. And you still have not learned how to prepare it properly. Instead of cooking the noble bird in a rich *mole*, you are more than likely to smother its dry meat with tomato ketchup. As you pour the sauce, *señora*, do you ever pause to contemplate the fate of those who first cultivated the *tomatl*? Would it disturb you to learn that they were squeezed to a bloody pulp for the sake of their golden pips? Or perhaps you innocently flavour the dull flesh with cranberries, courtesy of our brothers the Mohawks? Finally, let us not forget the roast potatoes, plundered from the Incas.

However, there is one custom you could never emulate in your civilized kingdom. It is this. The bloodthirsty conquistadors claimed that among the thirty or so bowls placed before Montezuma were some containing the flesh of young boys. You and your kind are too refined to be cannibals, is that not so, *señora*? Instead you come to steal our babies, as you once stole the infant Jesus from the Jews. You have no respect for history. Back in England you will call our little exiles Charles or Elizabeth and rob them of their birthright. So that they will become as English as your Christmas dinner.

When I next see Rosie she is weeping. Her lips are bloody and a tooth is broken. Rupert looks even worse, stretched full length on a sofa in the spacious lobby of the Hotel Majestic. 'Thank God,' she exclaims, 'a familiar face. Please help us.' How could I not? Just listen to her story. She was walking at dusk with Rupert, not many blocks from the *zócalo*, when a trio of drug-crazed robbers forced them into an old Pontiac. One sat beside her in the driver's seat pointing a gun at her head, while the other two got in the back and pistol-whipped Rupert. Somehow he found the strength to knock them both out. 'Run, Rosie,' he cried, jumping from the car. 'I didn't know what to do,' she says, 'the man with the gun told me that he would kill me if I tried to escape or even open my eyes. And there was Rupert begging me to run. He was asking me to do a big thing – to trust him with my life. In the end I did – with my eyes closed!'

It seems that I am wrong about Rupert. This is a man with plenty of *huevos*. As it is *la nochebuena* I decide to give him a present. 'Listen, my courageous friend,' I whisper in his ear, 'before Montezuma visited his wives he would drink *xocatl* from a golden cup. You call it chocolate, and weaken it with milk. Do as we do, take it dark and hot, and then give thanks to Quetzalcoatl, the gardener of paradise.'

My brother-in-law's surgery is in a small plaza near the railway station. Painted on the window is a list of his services. *Extraccíon sin dolor, Amalgama, Corona, Placa Total, Puente Fijo*, and *Presupesto* which is gratis. He also provides other more private duties while his patients are overcome by the sweetish odour of nitrous oxide. If the fancy takes him he may pick up an engraver's drill and perform scrimshaw upon the ivory shanks of a wisdom tooth. Or he may tattoo tiny insignia upon the buttocks of sleeping females. Sometimes, overcome by the beauty of the exposed parts, he forgets all about artistry (not to mention dentistry) and remembers only his manhood. Naturally I do not mention these other possibilities to Rosie as she gracefully succumbs to the laughing gas. Once she is unconscious I leave the room. My throbbing teeth make the sight of the extraction too personal.

And so when Rosie becomes pregnant – as she surely will – you must decide for yourselves whether it was due to the magic of the cacao bean, or the dirty realism of the dentist's chair.

Either way she is looking like a real *gringas rubias* on *las fiestas de navidad*, on Christmas Day itself. Much to my surprise she has accepted an invitation to share our meal. At midday I transport Rosie and Rupert from the colonial splendour of the Hotel Majestic to my more modest surroundings. 'Welcome,' says my wife, still wearing her apron. It has taken her many days to prepare the table, searching the markets for the fresh herbs and spices required for a real *mole poblano de guajolote;* for onion and garlic, for almonds and raisins, for cloves and cinnamon, for chocolate and tomato, for coriander, anise and sesame, not to mention three varieties of chili; *ancho, pasilla* and *mulato.* The bird itself was easier to find, being a former resident of our backyard.

Only after all the preliminaries have been completed can the cooking begin. In addition to the main course my wife has also produced *guacamole,* chicken consommé, salted cod, *arroz à la mexicana,* a salad containing beetroot, bananas, pineapple, oranges, peanuts, pomegranate, lettuce, and *jica-mas;* and finally, for dessert, sweet *tamales* flavoured with strawberries and honey in the manner favoured by Montezuma.

I introduce Rosie and Rupert to our numerous offspring and show them to their places, while my wife carries in all the food. Dish after dish is placed on the table, where the dominant culinary hues of brown, yellow, and green are offset by candlelight and the scarlet flames of our home-grown poinsettia. Likewise the dark secrets of the sauces are balanced by more dulcet flushes that unexpectedly suffuse the mouth. Our guests eat with increasing abandon. 'Well,' I say, 'what do you think of Christmas in Mexico?'

'Intoxicating,' says Rosie.

'It's the real thing,' says Rupert. At which point there is a knock at the door. It is Jaime with a baby.

The Lady With The Laptop

IT IS FRIDAY, and I am at the airport waving a little flag, a one-man welcoming committee. There is a name on the flag. I survey the arrivals, trying to put a face to the name. I do not have much to go on, just one telephone conversation.

'How will I recognize you?' I asked. 'Do you have any distinguishing features?'

'I'll be the lady with the laptop,' the voice replied, chuckling.

'What is so funny?' I asked. Of course I like to hear women laugh, but only when I have made the joke.

'Nothing,' it said.

'In that case,' I replied indifferently. 'I'll take my leave until next Friday.'

'Not so fast,' it said. 'I want you to check that I have a nice room and to make sure that it overlooks the Nile.'

'Madam, you are mistaking me for a travel agent,' I replied. 'Your creature comforts are not my business.'

'Do it anyway,' it said, still giggling, 'and remember that I'll be the lady with the little Toshiba.'

I refused to bid a polite farewell to the minx. On the contrary, I slammed down the receiver. Everyone looked at me with respect, save our oleaginous supervisor, who rose from his chair and began to move in my direction. Let him come! *Je ne regrette rien.*

The arrogant madam obviously assumed that I was an oh-so-ignorant gippy who had never heard of Anton Chekhov. As it happens, I am well acquainted with 'The Lady with the Lap-dog' and, being a man of the theatre, have witnessed countless productions of Chekhov's melancholy dramas too. Enough! Why should I care what a strange woman thinks of me? Who is she anyway? Who is Chekhov, for that matter? Did he ever win the Nobel Prize, like our own Naguib Mahfouz? It is not in my nature to boast, but I have to tell you that I am personally acquainted with Mahfouz, or am at least the friend of a friend.

Shafik Sherif and I went to the same school. In our younger days, it was fashionable for wealthy families to send their sons to ersatz Etons. So Shafik and I were both packed off to St George's, near the British Embassy in Cairo's Garden City where we were tutored and tortured by ruddy-faced buggers with old English surnames and Spartan vices. Shafik shone, but I was more like the stars at midday, ever-present but invisible.

Thus it has continued ever since. Shafik prospers, while I labour. Shafik edits the literary pages of *Al-Ahram*, while I perform menial tasks for the Institute of Translation. As such, it is Shafik's privilege to serialize the novels of Mahfouz, even before they have appeared in hard covers. Not only does Mahfouz publish his fiction in *Al-Ahram*, he literally invents it in an office at the newspaper. According to Shafik, he turns up every day at about nine o'clock, having already scanned the early editions and taken morning coffee at the Café Ali Baba *en route*, and writes solidly until noon, whereupon he makes a modest exit, returning home to take a nap.

For years, Shafik had been saying, 'My dear chap, you simply must meet Mahfouz – the man is a national treasure,' without ever progressing to an introduction. So the summons to the Café de l'Opéra came as a complete surprise. When I arrived, Shafik was reading the old man a letter. Since Mahfouz is hard of hearing, the recitation was slow and clear, enabling all within earshot to grasp that the sender was none other than François Mitterrand, the President of France. '*Je vous adresse mes félicitations les plus chaleureuses,*' concluded Shafik sonorously, '*et vous prie de croire à mes sentiments très cordiaux.*'

'Thank you,' said Mahfouz, patting Shafik on the hand, 'your voice is like a bell.'

'Allow me to present my dear friend Yonnan Wassef,' said Shafik, turning to me.

'Your name is strangely familiar,' commented Mahfouz. 'Are you not the young man who wrote *Mourning Becomes Electrolux*?' I blushed and sat down, tongue-tied.

'He is indeed,' said Shafik, 'the very man who was hailed by wise critics as the author of the season's *chef d'oeuvre*, the saviour of Egyptian theatre.'

'They were wrong,' I snapped bitterly. 'It turned out that the theatre of the absurd was redundant in a country where bureaucracy is an art form.'

As I spoke, a coffee-pot alighted upon our low table like a copper toucan. Three cups followed in formation, as well as bowls of pralines, pistachios and a platter of Turkish delight.

'I am no theatre-goer, being deaf and half-blind,' said Mahfouz, 'but I do recall being intrigued by your play. Tell me, Mr Wassef, what possessed you to make a tragic hero of the humble vacuum cleaner?'

How could I resist?

'Mr Mahfouz,' I replied, 'I understand that you do not like to travel. Had you done so, you would surely have observed that whereas most airports are overflowing with luxury items such as camcorders and music centres, the duty-free shops at Cairo proudly display an infinite variety of vacuum cleaners.'

Shafik poured the coffee and offered the bon-bons; sweet-toothed Mahfouz took a handful of pralines. He chewed them thoughtfully and, as he did so, inclined his head towards me.

'Why is this?' I continued. 'The obvious answer is that Cairo is a dusty city, famously so. But I pondered the subject more deeply, trying to tease out the esoteric meaning. I began with the user. Modern woman, whatever she may say, remains dedicated to provocation and procreation; her sworn enemies are ugliness and decay. See how she stands before the looking-glass with her lipstick and her rouge, aiming to disguise time's depredations; see how she dusts every cranny of her chamber, determined to eliminate the physical evidence of erosion. But in a city like ours, where the past is ever-present, smothering us like desert sand, her struggle seems hopeless. Enter the hero! A brand-new Electrolux from Sweden. Efficient, phallic, built like a flame-thrower. It is love at first sight. Modernity woos and weds tradition. Woman may falter, but the machine is inexhaustible. Night and day, day and night, her brave Viking sucks up the dirt, the dross, the debris and the decay. He is the answer to her prayers! But, alas, our Nordic *Übermensch* has bitten off more than he can chew. Lungs clogged with the residue of desiccated hopes, the salty dust of lost lives, he begins to shed tears from his ducts.'

'But what are you saying about Cairo that we don't already know?' said Mahfouz.

'That it is a place where the phallus has been feminized,' I replied, 'transformed into a womb on wheels.'

'Yonnan is something of an El Sayed,' explained Shafik, referring to the infamous Don Juan dreamed up by Mahfouz. 'He is a dear man, but he is notorious for his bad behaviour towards women.'

Goodness knows what impression Mahfouz formed of me during that first encounter, but it couldn't have been too bad, because we continue to meet from time to time. To be frank, these encounters are the highlights of my life, unlike the all-too-frequent confrontations with my immediate superior; one of which occurred – you'll remember – immediately after my introduction to the woman I now await.

The hierarch paused before delivering his chastisement, merely to prolong his pleasure. He removed a silver box from his waistcoat pocket, opened it gingerly and extracted a pinch of maccabaw, which he placed in his snout and inhaled with a porcine snort. Raising his head, he inspected his domain with a dolorous eye. I was just another of his minions, condemned to toil in a vast office with a dozen other trapped souls. Our task? To translate the jewels of modern Egyptian letters into infidel tongues. It is painstaking and soul-destroying work, this casting of pearls before swine. That is why my colleagues were so excited by the heated exchange with the virago. 'Ditch the bitch,' was their unanimous advice. Only the slave-driver dissented. He leaned over me and sneezed, spraying my desk with attar of roses. 'What do you think you are playing at?' he cried. 'Where are your manners?'

'She thinks she is Cleopatra,' I replied, 'but I am no lackey. It is not my style to take orders from a woman.'

'The world is changing,' said my supervisor, 'and we must all alter our habits accordingly.'

'A woman is bad enough,' I protested, 'but a Jewess from Tel Aviv is beyond the pale. I have my pride.'

'Swallow it,' he advised.

IF BILE WERE a convertible currency, I would long since have become a billionaire. As it isn't, I spat the filthy stuff into the gutter as I pushed my way through the reeking Khan El-Khalili until, God be praised, I reached the café where Shafik awaited me. At last, I closed the door upon the hubbub of *hoi polloi* and entered an oasis where hubble-bubbles gargled like hot springs. The horrible day was done. Sweet aromas of tobacco, coffee and sweat combined to form a meaty brew that engulfed me in a masculine embrace. 'My dear fellow,' exclaimed Shafik, as soon as he caught sight of me, 'whatever is the matter? You look like you have lost a pound and found a penny.'

'That is exactly how I felt until this very moment,' I said, 'but the prospect of your company as well as that of your esteemed colleague fills me with relief.'

Naguib Mahfouz, looking very dapper in a Chairman Mao jacket, nodded in acknowledgement of my compliment. 'What an excitable fellow you are,' he pointed out. 'One minute you are soaring, borne aloft by wild fancies; the next you are in the very deepest of the dumps.'

'Mr Mahfouz,' I said, 'since my days as a dramaturge came to a premature end, I have earned my wages at the Institute of Translation. It is my punishment for failure.'

'Forgive me, Mr Wassef,' said Mahfouz, interrupting my flow, 'but you are forgetting that I was a civil servant for thirty-seven years.'

'That was different; you are a genius, you had your self-respect,' I explained. 'Besides, I doubt that you were ever subjected to the humiliations that are my daily bread. For instance, were you ever plucked from your desk and sub-contracted to another ministry? Turned from an academic drone into something even worse . . . a dogsbody?'

'What has occasioned this alarming metamorphosis?' asked Shafik.

'Don't you read your own paper?' I cried. 'Don't you know that next week our city will be hosting the UN conference on population? Fifteen thousand delegates are expected from all over the world. Meanwhile, our compatriots in the *Gema'a Islamiya* have threatened to slaughter the lot. If any actually turn up, they will require assistance. And

I have been conscripted. Officially I am listed as an interpreter, but unofficially I am expected to be a guide and escort as required.' I sipped my bitter coffee. 'No overtime will be paid, of that you can be sure.'

'Now I remember!' exclaimed Shafik, banging the table. 'This is the conference that has attracted the attention of a world-famous beauty, a *belle dame sans pareil*.' He plucked a piece of Turkish delight from a blue-and-white bowl and popped it in his mouth, dusting his lips with white sugar. 'My beloved Barbarella, better known as Jane Fonda of Hollywood,' he said, smacking his chops. 'What are you bellyaching about, you miserable fellow? There is not a man in Cairo who would not gladly swap places with you, myself included.'

'You inhabit a fantasy world,' I replied. 'I have as much chance of meeting her as I have of being the first man on Mars.'

'*Carpe diem*,' advised Shafik, already calculating his own prospects.

INSTEAD OF JANE FONDA, I am awaiting a woman who thinks I am a fool. At 11.45, the passengers on the Air Sinai flight from Tel Aviv begin to appear at passport control. I recognize her at once. She is of medium height, sports a beret, a white T-shirt, tight blue jeans and has – this is conclusive – a little Toshiba swaying from a shoulder-strap. She sees my pennant with her name upon it and nods. I approach her, bowing and smiling like a carpet-seller. 'The lady with the laptop, I presume.'

She doesn't know how to react; is this mockery, or

typical Egyptian hospitality? Later, I compound the confusion by requesting permission to park the minibus outside the airport mosque in order to recite the midday mantra. She looks at me in surprise. I am wearing a suit and tie. Is this a disguise? Has she fallen into the hands of a Muslim fundamentalist in mufti? She knows the mosque is swarming with fanatics who would drive her people into the sea, but she has a liberal heart and believes in religious freedom. 'Please,' she says, 'I have no wish to stand between you and your god.' To tell you the truth, I have not prayed for years. I am doing so today only in order to embarrass the Jewess.

Actually, it is far worse than she imagines. Even I am taken aback by the imam's smouldering ire. He prefaces his remarks with a pun: not *population*, but *copulation*. It is a pun, but it is not a joke. He consigns the conference and all its participants to the pit. 'A terrible punishment awaits us if the conference proceeds,' he wails. 'A plague will fall upon the land, there will be tempests, torrents and thunderbolts. Cars will be washed into the sea, planes will fall from the sky, trains will topple from their tracks. The fuel will spill and ignite, and our rivers will flow with fire. I see villages engulfed. I see the charred bodies of donkeys, goats and dogs. I hear the screams of the doomed as they are boiled alive in the steaming mud. I hear the survivors cry, 'There is only one God!' as they seek refuge in the mosque. It will truly be a Day of Judgement.'

'Stirring stuff,' comments my wife's cousin Samir, who sports a white robe that shines as if it were laundered in paradise. I regard my fellow worshippers bobbing up and down like dabbling ducks as they conclude their prayers and wonder if I don't have more in common with my enemy in the Toyota.

'It's like Fort Apache,' says the lady with the laptop as we enter the heavily guarded atrium of the Rameses Hilton. Yes and no. There are certainly scores of policemen in evidence, but they are mostly unarmed. This is probably a sensible precaution. Many are illiterate boys from the country who more likely than not support *Gema'a Islamiya* and wouldn't know whether to shoot the delegates or save them. The deputies themselves are a motley assembly. Looking around, it seems that all of them are trying to register simultaneously. Fortunately, I recognize the receptionist. It is my cousin Walid. We greet one another. 'This lady is my responsibility,' I say, handing him a few pounds. 'Please find her a nice room at once.' As it happens, the room does overlook the river. However, it is not yet ready. I have no alternative; I must invite the Israeli into the lounge for a coffee.

The place is full of fat cats from Saudi who fly north every August to enjoy the illicit pleasures of a laxer society. They drink, they gamble, they fornicate and they examine my companion from head to toe as she crosses the room. We find a quiet table in a corner, beneath a vainglorious relief chipped from an obscure tomb in the Valley of the Kings. A waitress brings our order on a large tray. My companion raises the steaming cup to her lips.

'What do you think of Cairo?' I enquire.

'It gives me a buzz,' she replies. 'Its arteries may be European, but its heart is Arab.' She means it as a compliment, of course, but I decide to take it otherwise, to punish her for her patronizing manner.

'You mean we're picturesque,' I snap. 'An exotic novelty to pep up the jaded appetites of the pan-Americans?'

'I'm not an American,' she says, 'I'm an Israeli.'

'Is there a difference?' I say.

'Why do you keep up the pretence that we don't exist?' she asks. 'After the peace treaty was signed, we flocked across the border like Joseph and his brothers. We wanted to find out all we could about our once and future neighbours. That was fifteen years ago. It's still one-way traffic. Why? Aren't you the least bit curious about us?'

'To be honest, we are not,' I reply. 'I know you find this lack of curiosity incomprehensible, thinking yourselves so fascinating, but to us, you are upstarts, not really worth our attention.'

'In that case, Mr Wassef,' she says, smiling, 'you probably don't want to hear what one of our finest playwrights thought of *Mourning Becomes Electrolux*.'

Despite my better judgement, my undernourished ego lurches for the bait like a starving salmon. 'You mean you've heard of my play,' I gasp, 'in Israel?'

'Sure,' she says, beginning to reel me in. 'Our home-grown Ionesco came here a few years ago. He's an eccentric fellow. Some even call him perverse. In my opinion, they have a point. Did he visit the pyramids or King Tut's treasure? Not him! All he wanted to go to was an abattoir – don't ask me why – and the theatre. He saw half a dozen plays and hated them all. Save one.'

'Mine?' I ask.

'Yours,' she replies. 'In his judgement, it has the potential to be a great movie. He called you the new Buñuel.'

The movies! The Jews know how to do two things well: they know how to complain, and they know how to make films. Perhaps there is hope for me, after all. I imagine coming home, a million-dollar contract in my hands, able to impress my wife at last. My wife is a dreadful snob. We married while still at the university, when it seemed that I had unlimited prospects. We had two boys in rapid succession, who now attend a German-run boarding-school. It costs a fortune to keep them there, but they show me no gratitude. Nor does my wife. She constantly belittles me. I tell her we would have more money if we sent our kids to an ordinary school. She won't hear of it. 'We are poor because you are a failure,' she says, 'not because our children are receiving a good education.' Is it any wonder that I spend most of my time out of the house: at work, or in the cafés with Shafik and his cronies, discussing the three els – literature, life, and love.

Once, during my fifteen minutes of glory, I was invited to the United States, to the famous Writers' Workshop at the University of Iowa. It was there that I met my first Israeli, the celebrated Palestinian writer Anton Shammas. But that is not why I mention my trip. No, I want to tell you about my excursion to Yellowstone, where I went with my wife and our two babies. Driving through the park in a rented limo, we suddenly came across a crowd of people, all reverently staring in the same direction. Naturally, we were curious. We stopped the car, and the host of good people, seeing the babes in our arms, parted to let us through. And then we saw the object of their adoration: not the Virgin Mary, but a moose. The great beast continued to drink obliviously from the silver stream.

Well, the same atmosphere of profound wonderment suddenly falls upon the vast lounge of the Rameses Hilton. All eyes – Saudi eyes, Egyptian eyes, Yankee eyes, French eyes, sub-Saharan eyes, Chinese eyes – are turned towards a figure that has just emerged from the undergrowth of extras. It is a celebrity. It is Jane Fonda.

She walks through the room as if unaware of the stares that are accompanying her. What panache! And then, as she passes me, our eyes meet. She registers my existence. It is not exactly a miracle, more a reward – my reward for attending midday prayers. I smile at the future star of *Mourning Becomes Electrolux*, but she is gone.

While we are still transfixed by this spectacle, another beautiful woman enters our field of vision. She is an Egyptian, dressed from top to toe in black. Her tight chador is spun from black silk, and her headpiece is a black turban. Only her eyes are visible. The lids are darkened with kohl, which emphasizes the supernatural translucence of her irises. She moves with the grace of a cheetah and is – sacrilege – sexier than Jane Fonda herself. She is escorted by a handsome young fellow, exquisitely dressed in the sort of clothes that you ask for by name. I recognize them as such, even if the names themselves are unknown to a poor Egyptian scribe. He is obviously wealthy but also, I am glad to note, beginning to grow fat. In the years to come, he will surely lose the ability to contain her wildness.

'She's a real beauty,' whispers the Israeli.

'You are not unattractive yourself,' I reply, obviously inebriated by the moment.

'Tell me, Mr Wassef,' says the Israeli, ignoring my remark, 'do you think she is circumcised?'

'THERE ARE THREE types of female circumcision,' asserts Aziza Hussein, the notorious president of the Cairo Family Planning Association. 'First, there is the slight cut; second, the cut that removes part of the girl's clitoris; and third, the worst of them all, the pharaonic cut in which all the girl's genital organs are excised. The operation is usually performed by the village barber without the benefit of anaesthetic. His tools are the tools of his trade: scissors and razor. This assumes that the girl is lucky; most have the misfortune to be worked upon with broken glass or a slice of tin.' The assorted harpie – black harpies, yellow harpies, red harpies, white harpies, but all harpies – shake their heads in horror. Oh, the pity of it! Their collective self-righteousness fills the room like a bad odour.

'It is estimated that thirty per cent of the girls who suffer complications are left to die of so-called heart attacks,' continues Dr Aziza. 'When I ask mothers why they do this to their daughters, they tell me: "It is tradition." And it is. A shameful tradition that predates Islam. It survives because parents still believe that circumcision will protect a girl's virginity, dampen her libido, stop her running after men. Deep down, they are convinced that no decent Egyptian will marry a girl who is not circumcised. The tragedy is that the effects do not wear off after she is wed; she cannot enjoy sex before marriage, nor does she take any pleasure in it after.'

How does she know? Has she been speaking to my wife? Monday has dawned, and I am a reluctant participant in a seminar sponsored by the Society for the Prevention of Traditional Practices Harmful to Woman and Child. The Israeli woman sits tapping at the keyboard of her little Toshiba, occasionally looking to me for enlightenment when our native tongue is used. What am I to her? Nothing more than a useful adjunct to her machine. As I translate yet another phrase into the lingua franca, I remind myself why it is necessary to go on hating the Israelis. It has little to do with their Jewishness (though that is hardly to their advantage), but everything to do with their espousal – nay, their creation – of the modern world. They are like a bacillus in the body politic, and more and more of our people are being infected, especially the women. Do you really believe that Dr Aziza dreamt up her campaign against female circumcision all on her own? No, it does not smell Egyptian. You can be sure that the poison was first poured into her ear by her liberated sisters from over the border.

'Mr Wassef,' complains the lady with the laptop, 'you are losing concentration. I am missing too many of the contributions from the floor.' Oh, if I had the power I should drive her back across the Suez Canal. In 1973, the Third Army made a glorious assault upon the Israeli bunkers and restored our national pride. Would that I could do the same for our manhood. Instead, I am compelled to listen to this alien propaganda in the heart of our capital. Tell me, how would the Israelis like it if a group of cocksure crusaders suddenly turned up in their country determined to put an end to the age-old practice of male circumcision and set about denouncing the practitioners as barbaric baby-mutilators or worse? Well, we don't like it either.

At the end of the meeting, the local doctors, health-workers and teachers, the do-gooders who enter the middens and the villages to stamp out the abhorrent practice – quislings all – strut upon the stage and receive a standing ovation. Anyone would think they were war heroes. Then there is a great display of hugging, weeping and other sisterly emotion, as well as a mass exchange of *cartes de visites*.

Afterwards, we walk in silence along the corniche and watch the feluccas cross the river. Men and women lean together on the parapets waiting for the sun to sink between the hotels and the palms on the far bank. The air is rosy. It is a time for old-fashioned romance, a mood that is certainly foreign to my narrow-minded companion.

'Mr Wassef,' she says, regarding the Nile in its twilit beauty, 'are there such things as *bateaux mouches* in Cairo?'

'Certainly,' I reply.

'In that case,' she says, 'I'd like to have dinner on one. Can you arrange it for me? Better yet, can you join me?'

I want to tell her what to do with her invitation but then I think: why not? My wife was in a foul mood when I left this morning, her tongue as sharp as horseradish. I am in no great hurry to see her again. So it is to spite my wife, rather than humour the Israeli, that I accede to the latter's request.

DO I NEED to tell you that the boat is full of tourists? Mainly ubiquitous Saudis and émigrés from America who have made their pile and want the suckers in the old country to know it. They prance around in their grave goods: gold chains about their necks and chunky bejewelled rings on their fingers, like tiny quoits of silver. The women are even more vulgar, and their children are inevitably overweight. The *Topaz* is truly a ship of fools, a ship whose only cargo is kitsch.

On a platform in the dining room, a group of musicians in Hawaiian shirts are playing tunes that make me want to block my ears with beeswax. Why has the Israeli chosen this, of all places, to dine? Can it be that she wishes to humiliate me still further? To rub my nose in this gross parody of Egyptian-ness?

A waiter approaches our table and asks if we require anything to drink. 'Of course,' says the Israeli.

'Bring us a bottle of Cru des Ptolémées,' I say, 'the Pinot Blanc for preference.'

Meanwhile, we pile our plates with provisions from the buffet, scooping up mounds of humus, tahina, aubergine, wild rice, fish, and more. The outlandish guitarists disappear to be replaced by local boys. We fill our bellies and befuddle our brains with an excess of food and wine. And all the while, the ship glides down the Nile, the moving buckle on a girdle of light. To my astonishment, I realize that I am beginning to enjoy myself.

Then the drumbeats grow more insistent, and a whirling dervish makes his entrance. He is dressed all in white, save for his skirts, which are as brightly coloured as a spinning-top. He rotates for thirty minutes, as if perpetual motion were his natural state. Slightly green, he staggers below stairs to be replaced by a belly-dancer, who comes wriggling out in a sequin-studded brassière and transparent pantaloons. 'Behold, the latter-day Eve,' says the woman from Israel, 'who knows but one thing: how to move provocatively. Whereas her counterpart, the latter-day Adam, is mobility personified. The first is a prisoner, the second is a free man.'

'Come, come,' I say, 'this is merely a floor show. Don't you think you are taking it a bit too seriously?'

At which point, the Israeli shatters the mood completely by gathering up her laptop and crying: 'Do you want me to show you the figures? For too long women have been denied the same rights and opportunities as men, with devastating consequences to our health and well-being. That injustice is the real reason for our presence in Cairo – gender equality, nay the *empowerment* of women!' Why can't she behave like a date? Why is she so determined to politicize everything, including belly-dancing?

Besides, she is completely wrong. Women in need of empowerment? Not in Cairo, nor in Jerusalem, I'll venture. Just watch the belly-dancer as she swerves from table to table. See how the cowed men grab their wives lest she plucks them from their chairs and forces them to perform publicly with her. Tell me, who is in the ascendancy here? The drums are now pounding faster and faster, and the dancer's hips are playing push-me-pull-you. She is so close I can hear her rapid breathing, feel the warmth of her flesh. She orbits around me like a heavenly body, until her gravitational pull begins to shift me in my seat. I am being sucked unwillingly into the maw of her dance.

For some reason, our struggle has claimed the attention of the entire room, which now fills with yells of encouragement. I sense that my resistance is at an end, that I will be lifted from my place by an all-conquering force. What is one more humiliation in an age of humiliations? I prepare to bow to the inevitable. At which point the Israeli also rises and says: 'Leave him, I'll dance with you instead.' The crowd don't care; any victim will suffice.

They clap on the beat as the Israeli starts to sway to the sinuous rhythms. Soon, the music is dictating all her movements, as though her will were nothing but a metronome. She is possessed by the music, by the siren sounds of Cairo, and spontaneously raises her T-shirt to expose her belly-button, which contains no jewel save a glittering droplet of sweat. For a few delirious moments, I become convinced that she will bare her breasts, and joyously anticipate the shame that sober reflection will bring. Why should I feel gratitude to a prissy madam who is – like all her kind – a slut at heart? By the end, the pair of them – the hypocrite and the object of her scorn – are moving in unison like Siamese twins.

'That wasn't the first time you've done that,' I say accusingly when she resumes her seat.

'I won't deny it,' she replies, gasping for breath. 'I took lessons and sometimes dance at home.'

'So what gives you the right to criticize someone who has no choice but to do it for a living?' I ask.

'For a start,' she replies, 'I was attacking society, not the woman; and second, I studied belly-dancing to facilitate childbirth, not to provoke men.'

This takes me by surprise. I suppose I had assumed that all the women at a conference on population control would at least be childless, if not outright lesbians.

'You have children?' I ask.

'Two,' she replies. 'Two boys aged five and nine.'

'Yet again the practice seems at variance with the preaching,' I say.

'Not at all,' she replies. 'We decided that it would be irresponsible to have more than two children. And so, after the birth of the second, we shut the stable door. My husband had a vasectomy.'

What is there left to say? I simply stare at her in amazement. This Amazon is more dangerous even than I suspected. Egyptian women are bad enough, but they have never yet, so far as I know, demanded the emasculation of their husbands.

TWO DAYS LATER, to Shafik's chagrin, I'm flying down to Luxor with Jane Fonda. To be sure, we are not alone. On the contrary, we are accompanied by the mustachioed Minister of Tourism himself, a gaggle of his grey-suited minions, hotel owners, airline officials, as well as a flamboyant array of local actors (among them the leading man of *Mourning Becomes Electrolux*, now a bigshot, who cruelly refuses to acknowledge my presence), not to mention a score or more of the delegates (including Little Miss Sourpuss from Jerusalem). Two air-conditioned coaches, flanked by black-coated outriders, transport us to the Winter Palace Hotel on the bank of the Nile.

A few tourists sit on the veranda, gingerly sipping

brightly coloured fruit cordials and poring over maps of Upper Egypt in search of unseen treasures. They look up in astonishment as our entourage sweeps past. A flunkey in a chocolate-brown jacket with gold buttons and braid fusses obsequiously around the Minister. It has been a long journey, and Jane Fonda is obviously uncomfortable.

'Hey,' she says to the flunkey, 'where's the restroom round here?'

'You have a choice,' he replies, gliding over the marble floor. 'Here we have the Continental Brasserie, for steak and chips, and, over there, the Oriental Terrace, where more traditional dishes are served.'

'The man is a numskull,' mutters the actress with the distended bladder. I seize my opportunity, almost without premeditation. 'Fool,' I cry, pushing the menial aside. 'Miss Fonda asked for a restroom, not a restaurant. Please,' I say, addressing the prima donna, 'allow me to guide you.'

'Why, thank you,' says Jane Fonda, walking with some haste. I calculate that I have no more than thirty seconds in which to sell my script.

'You may be surprised to learn this,' I say, 'but I am the man who wrote the most successful play of 1988. It ran for fifteen months on Cairo's equivalent of Broadway. The good news is that I have just completed a version for the big screen. A version written with you in mind. What do you say, Miss Fonda? Can I send it to you? Will you read it?' My Omar Sharif eyes brim with tears, ready to overflow at the merest hint of an affirmative. A nod would suffice.

'Send it to my agent,' she replies, before disappearing into the ladies' room. At least she didn't say no.

When I return to the main corpus, I find that a middle-aged Englishman and his young daughter have engaged my Israeli in conversation. The girl is on the cusp of puberty, beauty in bud, but he looks devastated, as though he is convalescing from a heart attack, or worse. 'Tell me,' the man is saying, 'was that really Jane Fonda?'

'I think so,' the Israeli replies, as though a Hollywood star is unworthy of her attention.

'There's no doubt about it,' I say, butting in, 'that was indeed the one and only Jane Fonda.'

'Well I never,' says the Englishman, 'in Luxor of all places.'

'Daddy,' says his daughter, 'can you ask the man to get her autograph?'

'Ask him yourself,' I say, pinching her cheek. 'The man won't bite you.'

WE LEAVE THE Winter Palace before dawn and troop down to the quayside, where we board a boat that will ferry us across the Nile. The Englishman and his daughter are already on board. They wave to the Israeli, who takes a seat beside them. I settle in behind. They must have continued their conversation after I retired last night, for a rapport has already been established, suggesting that intimacies of some sort have been exchanged.

'I dreamt of my wife last night,' says the Englishman quietly. 'She would have been so excited to be doing this.' He stops, looks around and absentmindedly strokes his daughter's sun-bleached hair. 'She was a teacher, you know,' he continues, 'of history. I can picture her now, leaning on her desk, telling her kids the story of Howard Carter and the discovery of King Tut's tomb. I can see them, open-mouthed, as she describes how he found the first step, then fifteen more, then the doors, the last one with the unbroken seal. She was a great teacher. Knew how to hold a pause. When the kids could bear it no longer, she'd pretend she was looking through a keyhole and say: "I can see wonderful things."' I yawn loudly. I have heard it all before. I am more interested in rubbing the sleep from my gummy eyes.

A slight breeze, no more than a warm exhalation, causes the boat's cotton canopy to shiver. In the greater canopy, the night shift is just ending. The full moon is retiring to the west bank, the land of the dead, where it will pack away our dreams and secret desires, the succubi and the incubi, the vampires and the ghosts, for another twelve hours. Meanwhile, the sun is clocking in above Luxor, the city of light, the city of the living, setting fire to the palms and minarets. This celestial exchange is reflected in the immaculate meniscus of the river, which is scattered with chevrons of mercury and flame. A few ibises glide over the surface, disappearing to the south, where the waters widen. The Nile is the heart of our country. More! More! It is the very pivot of the world, the meeting point of night and day, life and death, the quotidian and the dark side of humanity.

My meditation is rudely concluded by the noisy arrival of six black limousines and their attendant guardian angels, all of whom sport halos of blue light and carry Kalashnikovs. Chauffeurs appear and, heads bowed, open doors. Out steps Jane Fonda, followed by lesser luminaries, various ministers, unrecognizable dignitaries and – if my eyes do not deceive me – the president's wife. All ascend the gangplank, like the seraphim in Jacob's dream.

The principals aboard, the overture complete, grimy dark-skinned fellows cast off the ropes, and the boat commences its journey to the other world, on whose shores derelict hovels bask in the reflected glory of the rising sun, their windows glinting with false life.

The Englishman is bowled over by the Valley of the Kings. 'We were slaves in Egypt once,' he says, 'and now we are tourists.'

So he is another Jew; merely an ersatz Englander, a bit like me. The Israeli laughs. She, too, is impressed. What Jane Fonda makes of it, I cannot say. I glimpse her only in the distance, shielded from the elements (and the likes of me) by Japanese umbrellas and muscular bodyguards.

'Mr Wassef,' enquires the Englishman's daughter, 'when will you be getting her autograph?'

Here we stand beneath heaven's hot blue flame, on the outer rim of a glowing honeycomb, each indentation filled with marvels, and all she can think about is the signature of an animated Barbie doll. I am tempted to slap her for insulting our ancient kingdom.

Wicked man, you will be thinking, hypocrite! Did you not put a greater value on her yea only yesterday? Ah, but that was self-interest, a different matter entirely; it was not Jane Fonda I cared about *per se*, only her power.

It is midday. In the fields, the fellahin loosen their djellabas and watch with rumbling bellies as their wives advance towards them through the swaying rows of *berseem* or sugar cane with bowls of *melokhia* balanced upon their heads. These peasants may not own a bean and be blessed with the intellects of donkeys, but they have loyal women. My wife serve me lunch? I'm lucky if she throws it at me. As it happens, we are offered the selfsame soup for our midday meal, though in somewhat different surroundings, and by waiters who do not carry the tureens on their heads.

The dusty plain that stands before the cliff-side temple of Hatshepsut is normally the province of the Polish National Academy of Sciences, but today it has been annexed by the Ministry of Tourism. Huge marquees, hundreds of metres in length, have been erected to provide shelter from the infernal sun. More discreet pavilions service baser requirements. Within the former, I feel like one of Pharaoh's charioteers who, having failed to catch Moses, finds himself at the bottom of the Red Sea. Here, sunshine is transformed by sumptuously coloured appliqués into cooling showers of saturated light that stain the face or fall straight upon the ochre ground, until it seems awash with red, yellow, blue and magenta. On either side, the banks of food swell and rise like coral reefs. Of course, there are fish; *samak Moussa* or sole, *loukoz* and *Sultan Ibrahim*, fried with *cousbareia* sauce.

It has become customary to serve *melokhia* at the start of such banquets because it is so unambiguously Egyptian; its unique mixture of indigenous leaf, garlic, oil, and stock being deemed admirably patriotic. This version, being for the rich, is beefed up with fried minced meat and chicken balls.

After that, we are faced with a veritable wall of poultry and game. There is chicken with vinegar; chicken with pomegranate sauce; chicken with rhubarb; chicken with quinces; chicken with plum jelly; chicken with mulberries; chicken with chickpeas, onion, and cinnamon. There are fowls in sweet stew: with *fistakiyyeh* or pistachios, with *wardiyeh* or rose-hips, with hazelnuts and julep, or perhaps with purslane, which is called *sott alnoubeh* or the Nubian woman, after its black appearance.

Chicken is ubiquitous, chicken is protean. Even the bread is stuffed with chicken. Otherwise there are pigeons and doves bursting with wild rice and pine kernels. After the birds come the eggs, great pyramids of eggs, *hamine* eggs, simmered for six hours with onion skins, until the whites have turned beige and the yolks a creamy yellow. As to vegetables ... what else but *ful medames*, for is it not said: 'Beans have satisfied even the pharaohs'? They are scooped up with ladles from vast earthenware vessels, buried deep in hot ashes and deposited into pockets of pitta. There are fine wines, cold beers and colas for foreigners to guzzle, while good Muslims can sip rose-water syrup or tamarind juice. Couches and divans are provided for the satiated or the sleepy.

NEEDLESS TO SAY, we were forced to read all the classic English texts at St George's: *Lorna Doone*, *Great Expectations*, *Prester John*, *King Solomon's Mines*, *The Children of the New Forest*, *Kim* and *Treasure Island*. Of course, I remember all the plots perfectly, but the only line that still sticks in my mind comes not from any of these, but from a letter Robert Louis Stevenson sent to his mother. 'An opera is far more real than real life to me,' he wrote. 'I wish that life was an opera.

I should like to *live* in one.' Hear, hear! Egypt should not be a land of fellahin, haute bourgeoisie and bureaucrats, but a country of fat men and Farouks, of divas and Cleopatras, a place far larger than life, a vast stage dedicated to opera. There are precedents. Didn't the Khedive commission Verdi to write an opera to celebrate the opening of the Suez Canal? And aren't we all here, before the temple of Hatshepsut, waiting for *Aida* to commence? Now you know the truth. It wasn't Jane Fonda who drew me down to Luxor, it was the prospect of seeing my favourite opera. This may sound unconvincing, coming from a dramatist manqué with absurdist tendencies. All I can tell you is that my interest in the avant-garde was like love on the rebound; if I couldn't have my prima donna I wouldn't settle for a chorus girl, so I went to the other extreme and courted Miss Anorexia instead.

Spears of light pick out the colonnades of the temple and the reliefs carved on the walls within. The conductor takes his bow, the orchestra springs to life, a mighty crescendo shakes the desert floor, thereby – or so it seems – reanimating the ancient figures inside the temple. Anyway, people emerge slowly from between the columns, as if newly summoned from a millennial slumber. Five hundred singers and dancers, all dressed in the manner of the ancients, perhaps the very courtiers and soldiers who accompanied Queen Hatshepsut on her famous expedition to Punt. And surely that overweight mezzo-soprano is none other than the grotesquely fat wife of the local chieftain they found there. I sit spellbound and weep at the end when Aida and Radames (played by my friend – well,

Shafik's friend – Hassan Kamy) sing their final duet, having been buried alive in a crypt by heartless priests. I observe that I am not the only one moved to tears as the great lament suffuses the night.

> *O terra, addio, addio, valle di pianti . . .*
> *Sogno di gaudio che in dolor svani.*
> *Ah! noi si schiude il ciel e l'alme erranti*
> *Volano al raggio dell'eterno di.*

Oh Earth, farewell, farewell vale of tears . . .
Dream of joy which vanished into sorrow.
Heaven opens towards us, and our wandering souls
Fly fast towards the light of eternal day.

The Englishman is hugging his daughter. Both are crying.

Before the last tear has dried, the air is filled with a new noise, accompanied by an artificial wind which causes our shirts to billow and our curls to unfurl. Helicopters are circling overhead, stirring the fields of sugar cane with spatulas of light. You don't need to be head of the *Mukhabarat* to guess who they are looking for. *Aida* was produced in such an extravagant manner to persuade tourists that Upper Egypt is perfectly safe, so it would be a source of great embarrassment if a member of *Gema'a Islamiya* were suddenly to pop up from the greensward and assassinate Jane Fonda or any other guest. 'We've got to fight these so-called fundamentalists,' booms the Minister of Tourism, as we return intact to the east bank, to the land of the living. 'We can't let them destroy our economy.'

●

'MR WASSEF, WOULD you do me a great favour?' asks the lady with the laptop as we dip our croissants in morning coffee at the Winter Palace Hotel. 'The Englishman and his daughter intend to revisit the Valley of the Kings this morning. They have asked me to accompany them. I should like to go, but I am afraid that my acceptance will be wrongly interpreted. "Yesterday was for my wife," he said, "but today is for me." What do you think he meant by that, Mr Wassef?'

'I really don't know,' I say, slicing a fig, 'but I have heard that the bereaved often spout nonsense.'

'Perhaps you are right,' she replies, 'but I fear that I may have raised false expectations in him, which I have no intention of realizing. Anyway, Mr Wassef, I should be terribly grateful if you could help me out by coming along. Your very presence will be sufficient to short-circuit any embarrassing incidents.'

'As it happens my wife's uncle owns the Memnon Papyrus Museum across the river,' I say. 'He has produced some wall-hangings for my two boys which are, by his own account, absolute masterpieces. Being a conscientious father, I promised to collect them if the opportunity arose.' I take a spoonful of yoghurt. 'Apparently it has. Should you and your companions also stop there briefly and even make a few purchases – you can have your name written in hieroglyphics while you wait – I shall definitely find myself in my wife's good books when I return home.'

'You surprise me, Mr Wassef,' says the lady with the laptop, 'I really didn't see you as a family man.'

'If you will excuse me,' I say, rising from the table, 'I must make a telephone call. To alert my wife's uncle of our imminent arrival.'

The Englishman does indeed seem disappointed by my presence, but he hides it well. Like me, he has been taught to dissemble by masters. His daughter, however, is unable to conceal her pique when I confess that I have not yet been able to obtain Jane Fonda's autograph. We are ambling along the corniche in the direction of the ferry. The sun has long since risen, and the river, a dazzling blue, seems to be spawning phosphorescent fish. A witches' brew of diesel and dung drifts over from the boulevard, sweetened en route by oleander, frangipani, and jacaranda. The road is busy but uncannily quiet. Phaetons pulled by starving nags move slowly, mechanically, like half-wound clockwork toys. Even the cars seem to be drifting in dreamy slow motion. Rich tourists in crumpled linen suits and cotton frocks clutch their bottles of mineral water and mop their brows with spotted handkerchiefs, while local greybeards slump on benches beneath the palms like basking seals. Everyone seems overcome by lassitude, as though battling with the heat has worn them out. 'You know what,' says the Englishman, 'Luxor reminds me of Yalta or somewhere like it. Not that I've been there,' he adds. 'But I have read Chekhov.' That man again! Why can't anyone view our country through Egyptian eyes?

'Chekhov?' says his daughter. 'Isn't he that silly character in *Star Trek*?'

'I suspect your daddy's thinking of a different Chekhov,' I say, looking at the Israeli, 'a Russian writer who wrote some world-famous stories.'

Our driver is waiting for us on the opposite bank. I explain that there has been a slight change of plan. He shrugs. What's it to him? We set off in the direction of the Theban Hills. Within minutes, we have reached our first destination, the Colossi of Memnon: monstrous survivors from antiquity, who sit there like diners in a deserted restaurant, their gargantuan appetites for ever unsatisfied. The driver steers the minibus into the car park. An elderly policeman with a huge moustache and the bearing of a sergeant-major leans against the window and extracts some baksheesh. 'According to Strabo, the northern colossus used to emit a soft, bell-like sound at dawn,' says the Englishman. 'The Greeks thought it was in mourning.'

'For what?' asks his daughter.

'For life, I suppose,' he replies. The man is obsessed!

The Israeli picks up her laptop, hoists it on her shoulder, then freezes like a wild animal that has been startled. 'What's that noise?' she asks. A good question! If it were winter, I'd say that hailstones were falling on the bus, but it is August, and there is not a cloud in the sky. Before I can produce an alternative hypothesis, the windscreen disintegrates, showering us with shards of glass. The little girl screams.

'Down!' cries the policeman. 'Everyone down on the floor.' He rolls under the bus. I look out of the window and observe three men in white robes running towards us across a brilliant green field of *berseem*. They are howling like berserkers and, far worse, brandishing Kalashnikovs.

I am mystifed by my response, which is completely out of character. I do not run for my life. Instead, as the bullets begin to tear into the side of the vehicle, I instinctively fling myself upon the Israeli woman, interceding between her and mortal danger. Don't ask me why! Perhaps I am inspired by the Englishman, who is all but smothering his daughter. Or perhaps I am simply performing what man has been programmed to do in such circumstances. We dare not move; we hardly dare breathe; we feel as vulnerable as ears of wheat when the locusts come. In fact, I am still covering the lady with the laptop when the cop opens the door and announces that the would-be assassins have vanished.

'Is everyone all right?' he enquires.

I help the Israeli to her feet. She is unscathed, but there are two neat holes in her Toshiba. The machine dies quietly. No flashes as it reverts to its inanimate state, no hissing as the memory absconds. 'I have lost everything,' she wails, hugging the machine, 'every word I have written since I arrived in Egypt. My notes? Gone! My statistics? Gone! My new ideas? Gone! My . . .'

She is about to continue her lamentation when she sees the sight that has rendered the rest of us speechless. The Englishman is holding his daughter in his arms. A splinter of glass, the size of a playing card, is embedded in her forehead. Her face is white, save for a contour line of red around the wound, which looks like a mouth with a transparent tongue vulgarly on show.

'Oh, I must have done something terrible to deserve this,' wails her father, 'but for the life of me, I cannot think what. After the funeral, my comforters assured me that the worst was over, but I knew better. I had the feeling that something like this would happen. I sensed that He was still holding my daughter hostage. I could almost hear Him say, "One false move, and the kid gets it!"'

'Who are you talking about?' I say.

'God, of course,' he says, 'my enemy.'

'No,' I say, 'neither Jehovah nor Allah, but the latter's self-appointed agents on earth. In other words, some gentlemen from *Gema'a Islamiya*.'

Meanwhile, the Israeli raises the erstwhile laptop above her head and hurls it through the broken window, as Moses once cast aside the Ten Commandments. I note that her armpits are smooth and hairless. Ah, so she is not ideologically pure after all. Red with shame, she approaches the Englishman and his melancholy burden. 'I don't know what to say,' she mumbles, touching his arm.

He stands immobile, like some modern-day *pietà*. 'She's gone for ever,' he whispers, 'as dead as earth.'

The Israeli stares down at the girl's face. 'You're wrong!' she cries. 'She is not dead! She is in shock, for sure. But she is not dead. Look at the glass.' Sure enough, small beads of condensation trickle down its underside, as miraculous as the tears of the Virgin.

'If only you are right,' says the Englishman, 'then all my sorrows may yet be redeemed.'

The entire staff of the Memnon Papyrus Museum are lined up on the porch, my wife's uncle to the forefront. 'Do not worry!' he yells as, led by the driver, we stumble from the wreckage into the uncanny stillness of an otherwise ordinary day. 'Do not worry! I have informed the authorities. Help is already on the way.' Then he recognizes me and can barely contain his amazement. 'Yonnan, is it you?' he cries. 'Why are you here and not in Cairo?' He clasps a hand to his forehead. 'Allah protect me!' he moans. 'The boy has brought bad news.' He is an old man, his memory is not what it was. I remind him that I have come, as arranged, to collect the gifts for my sons. 'Of course,' he mutters. Still looking perplexed, he hugs me. 'Such a terrible thing, Yonnan,' he wails, 'and that it should happen outside my shop.'

The police also regard the incident as tactless, if not downright inconsiderate, coming so soon after *Aida*'s open-ing night. And, in the absence of the actual perpetrators, they are inclined to hold us responsible. 'Why did you not inform the local police of this excursion?' asks an officer accusingly. 'They would have ensured your safety. If you had only told them in advance, this poor girl would still be in the pink.' The aforementioned victim is surrounded by young men in dirty djellabas, each of whom seems deter-mined to pluck the splinter from her skull, as if she were the afflicted heroine of some fairy story and her father a rich king committed to rewarding the man who first awakens her. Anyway, the general consensus is that the glass should be removed as quickly as possible. The English-man, however, has the casting vote. 'Let her be,' he commands, holding her tightly to his chest, 'the doctors will decide.'

It takes fifteen minutes for a helicopter to remove us from the land of the dead and deliver us to the halfway house they call the Luxor Hospital for Fevers. I can feel the Englishman's confidence in the local medicos begin to waver as soon as he sees the crudely painted sign at the hospital's entrance. It disappears altogether when we enter the building proper. This is no place for the living; it is limbo-land, and its inhabitants are the moribund and their lachrymose acolytes.

The hot and stinking corridor is chock-a-block with the latter; keening women in shabby burnouses. The Englishman sidesteps them with a finesse I haven't seen since I played rugger at St George's. Actually, he has no choice, given that he has chosen to keep pace with his daughter, now supine on a trolley, hanging on to her limp hand while a pair of scruffy porters wheel her at breakneck speed in the direction of the X-ray room. The purpose of the X-ray is to define the damage, to discern how deeply the glass has penetrated the brain. The question is this: are we now looking at the whole iceberg, or merely its tip?

IF YOU HAVE ever had the misfortune to travel with the lower classes on an Egyptian train, you will be familiar with the waiting room. The place is filthy, the air foul. Crumpled packets of cigarettes litter the floor. Glasses of sweet tea stand half-finished on scratched tabletops. Some have been there so long, judging by the number of drowned flies, they are topped with black foam. Unwashed fellahin snooze horizontally on the benches, while their wives prepare food over little paraffin stoves. Worst of all are the children, verminous little brats who wail or run about like cockroaches. In a matter of moments, I am converted to the cause of population control, to the use of contraceptives, with especial emphasis upon abortion. So why am I still

here with the groundlings? Why haven't I returned to my
rightful place among the luminaries at the Winter Palace
Hotel? What do I care about a foolish little girl whose only
ambition in life seems to be the acquisition of Jane Fonda's
autograph? What is the matter with me?

'She looks just like my wife,' says the Englishman, 'same
fine features, same charming smile. To tell you the truth,
when I saw her on the trolley outside the operating theatre,
I thought she *was* my wife. I suppose you'd better call it
déjà-vu rather than mistaken identity.' He cannot keep
quiet, let alone sit still. 'You see,' he continues, 'I've done all
this before. At the beginning of the year – what's that, eight
months ago? – I waited six hours while they cut a tumour
the size of a tangerine out of my wife. Now it's my
daughter's turn. Her doctor is very optimistic. He tells me
that I'm not to worry. He assures me – in excellent English
– that the X-rays are fine, that the injury is not as bad as it
looks, that the glass can be extracted without fear of the
consequences. A piece of cake, he calls it. My wife was also
offered an excellent prognosis. A sixty per cent chance of a
full recovery, which, believe me, is music to the ears of a
person with cancer. Sure enough, she recovered well from
the surgery. They had her on her feet within days. But
shortly afterwards, things started to go wrong. The wound
opened and wouldn't stop weeping. Her bowels ceased to
function. Her belly distended. And one night, on the
commode, she passed out. The nurses panicked. They got
her back on the bed and fitted her up with an oxygen mask.
That's how I found her; her bald head uncovered, her
eyelids fluttering, her skin as white as a hard-boiled egg.

The houseman came running – a woman from Hong Kong with all the humanity of a Red Guard, she shooed me away, examined my wife, then asked to see me in her office. 'The pulse is strong, the heart is good,' she said indifferently. 'I don't think she is nearing the end.' Dying? Who said anything about dying? My wife was supposed to be getting better, not dying. Later, other doctors succeeded in reassuring me, but I couldn't get those words out of my mind. Indeed, they proved prophetic; that episode turned out to be a dress rehearsal for the real thing. And now history is repeating itself.'

'You sound like one of those sick Jews who believes that it is his destiny to suffer, to be one of history's perennial victims,' snaps the Israeli. 'But I am here to tell you that it need not be so. Your wife died, and I sympathize. But it doesn't follow that your daughter will too.'

'I'm sorry if I'm letting the side down,' says the Englishman, 'but I wonder how rational you'd be if it was your daughter in there.'

'Point taken,' says the Israeli. 'In fact, my husband's probably going haywire right now if he's heard news of the attack and had no reassuring word from me on e-mail. You probably didn't notice, but my laptop was the other casualty of the attack.' She lowers her voice and addresses me in a manner that, in other circumstances, would be described as intimate. 'I'd telephone him,' she whispers, 'but I think my place is here for the moment. Just in case I'm wrong.'

'Give me the number,' I say, 'and I'll have my office contact him immediately.' She scribbles some figures on a scrap of paper which she hands to me. I pocket it and depart in search of a phone. When I return, she is all alone.

'Someone in a white coat appeared and led the English-man away,' she explains.

'TELL ME,' SAYS my friend Shafik, lounging on a divan at the brand-new Café de Luxe, 'how was Luxor? Did you meet Jane Fonda?' He toys with some marzipan. 'Did you screw her? Come on, Yonnan, spill the beans.'

'Are you teasing me, Shafik?' I say. 'Or are you really an ostrich? Surely there were a few lines in *Al-Ahram* about the ambush.'

'Not a dicky-bird, old chap,' he replies. 'According to our ace reporters, everything was as smooth as silk, not so much as a single shot fired in anger.'

I shrug. Obviously, the authorities, in their wisdom, decided that such a minor fracas, nothing more than an 'isolated incident', was hardly worth mentioning to the press. I am about to enlighten Shafik when a waiter approaches our table and won't go away. 'What does he want?' I ask. 'Don't worry, he's not with the *Mukhabarat*,' laughs Shafik. So I commence my narrative.

Meanwhile, the dextrous waiter drops a lump of wax into a coffee-pot, which he places on a portable stove. 'That's the ambergris,' says Shafik. 'When it is melted, he will pour in the coffee. Then he will fumigate our cups with smoulder-ing embers of mastic.'

'Anyway,' I say, 'the girl survived the operation. After-wards, her father was very keen to fly her back to England, or even Israel, but the British Consul insisted that there were cheaper options. 'The private hospitals in Cairo are perfectly adequate,' he said. In the end, she was transferred to the El Fayrouz Clinic in Giza. For some reason, I chose to accompany the Englishman and the Israeli when they moved the girl, perhaps because I was in no hurry to return home. The girl travelled in an ambulance, of course. We shared a taxi. The driver took us the long way, over the Sixth of October Bridge. Did he do it maliciously, knowing that one of his passengers was an Israeli? If so, he hit the wrong target. The Englishman, not the Israeli, reacted. 'The sixth of October 1973, that's a day I'll never forget,' he mused. 'In the afternoon, a friend comes running around – have I heard the news? The Egyptians have crossed the Suez Canal. The Syrians are swarming over the Golan Heights. The situation is desperate. A few moments later, the phone rings. A woman friend. She is at a party in York. Would I like to join her? It's Yom Kippur, I'm in London and I'm worried about Israel's survival, but I say yes. Yes! Yes! As soon as the fast ends, I shoot up the motorway. I arrive in York just before midnight. She is clearly pleased to see me. We embrace. We talk. Hold hands. Kiss. Smoke marijuana. And make love. To you, this bridge may commemorate a war, but for me, it is a reminder of the first time I made love to my wife.' Poor fellow! The whole world is a memorandum that his beloved once existed and that he has lost her.'

'What a story!' exclaims Shafik. 'Does it have a happy ending? Will the girl recover? Will the hero get his proper reward? I trust that the lady in question has already demonstrated her gratitude.'

'The girl is still unconscious,' I reply, 'but not in a coma, the doctors insist, just deeply asleep. As for the Israeli, she hasn't even said thank you.'

'The ungrateful bitch,' says Shafik.

At last, the waiter departs. Shafik sips the fragrant brew. 'Apparently, the owner went to Japan and fell in love with the tea ceremony they have over there,' he explains. 'Upon returning, she resolved to establish an equivalent in Egypt. What do you think?'

'The tourists will love it,' I say, 'but I cannot see Naguib Mahfouz becoming a regular.'

Now it is Shafik's turn to surprise me. 'Haven't you heard?' he says, putting down his coffee cup. 'Mahfouz is in hospital.'

'Since when?' I say.

'Since yesterday,' replies Shafik. 'He was walking home from one of his haunts when he was accosted by a group of fanatics, one of whom stabbed him in the neck.'

The news shocks me more than the attempt on my own life (which had the merit of being impersonal). What sort of country is it if our greatest writer cannot walk the streets in safety? Maybe the Israeli was right when she said that the war was no longer between Jew and Arab, but between progressives and fundamentalists.

THE CONFERENCE ENDS, and the delegates pack their bags. I return to my post at the Institute of Translation. I am there, slouched over my desk, when the Israeli unexpectedly telephones. Needless to say, we do not have individual receivers, so it is our taskmaster who takes the call. 'Keep it brief,' he hisses.

'Good news,' says the Israeli. 'The girl has woken up.'

'Wonderful,' I say (and, what's more, I mean it).

'She is asking for you,' continues the Israeli.

'For me?' I say.

'Yes,' comes the reply. 'She wants to know whether you managed to obtain Jane Fonda's autograph.'

'It was the last thing on my mind,' I say.

'No matter,' says the Israeli. 'I have a plan.'

THE CO-CONSPIRATORS MEET at lunchtime in the lobby of the El Fayrouz Clinic, mingling with its 152 resident professors and consultants. 'What do you think of this?' asks the Israeli. She hands me a piece of card. Written on it are the words: TO A BRAVE LITTLE GIRL, WITH LOVE FROM YOUR FRIEND, JANE FONDA.

'You are a genius,' I cry. 'How did you get it?'

'Well,' says the Israeli, looking pleased with herself, 'I remembered that Jane Fonda had sent a letter of solidarity to every delegate at the conference. So it was just a matter of unearthing the original and copying the signature.' She places the two side by side.

'Brilliant,' I say. 'Even Jane Fonda couldn't tell them apart.'

Nor, Allah be praised, can the girl. 'Mr Wassef,' she says, 'how can I thank you?'

'By getting better,' I say, kissing the plaster on her forehead, 'and by remembering that many more Egyptians wished you well than did you harm.' The Englishman beams and shakes my hand.

'That girl made me ashamed,' says the Israeli as we step out onto Gamal Salem Street. 'She sheds tears of gratitude for a forgery, while I haven't even thanked you properly for a genuine act of courage. It is possible that you saved my life, Mr Wassef. The least I can do in return is to buy you dinner at my hotel. Not tonight. Tonight I am dining with the Englishman. Perhaps tomorrow?'

'YESTERDAY WAS AN extraordinary day,' announces the Israeli as she sips her ice-cold vodka. 'Just before sunset, the Englishman knocked on my door — we have adjoining rooms — and asked if I would care to accompany him to the pyramids. You can see them from our hotel bedrooms, but they are further away than they look. So we took a taxi. It was dusk when we arrived, and all the tourists had departed, but not the guides. "You must have a guide," said one, more persistent than most. "They insist. No entry without. You want camel? You want horse? I give you very quiet horse." We followed obediently, not knowing better. The stables stank of dung. Those horses that were not tethered were being whipped. Everyone had whips. If they had no horses to whip, they whipped the air. Our mounts looked half-starved. "Off you go," commanded their owner, throwing stones at their flanks, "tally ho!" They trotted up the hill, wheezing like asthmatics. We felt guilty to be adding to their burdens.' She finishes her vodka and orders another. I ask for a whisky. The Israeli looks at me quizzically. 'So you are not such a good Muslim after all,' she says. 'The flesh is weak,' I reply, 'especially if the spirit is strong.'

'The whole place now belonged to the locals,' she continues. 'Wild youths galloped their emaciated nags across the dunes, while their elders led the camels to wherever camels go at night. First the sky was pink, then pale blue, then a darker blue, as if the heavens were slowly freezing over. Whole families unrolled rugs and squatted at the base of the pyramids, where they prepared and ate their supper. What can I say? It was a magnificent sight. It stirred my blood. The Englishman, however, was very quiet. "A penny for your thoughts," I said. "I was thinking about the last time I kissed my wife," he said. I leaned across and patted his thigh, which was the best I could do in the circumstances. Actually I wanted to hug the poor man, to restore him to the present, so that he too could partake of the extraordinary atmosphere. But he was lost in some distant cancer ward.

'"It was the last Friday of her life," he said. "By then, the pain had become unbearable, and she was sedated most of the time. Not exactly asleep, but not entirely conscious either. On that day, alarming new symptoms began to appear. She became paranoid, imagined that everyone in the ward was plotting against her. She got angry if I tried to speak. 'Hush,' she would say, 'can't you see I'm listening?' Things got worse very rapidly. She began talking to herself. Nonsense, gibberish. Even more upsetting was the look of terror that haunted her eyes. You are familiar with the phrase, 'scared out of her wits'? Well, I was looking at its personification. Hitherto, I had always been able to calm her, but not that Friday. She had moved beyond my reach. So she lay there in her bed, a living skeleton with a quivering jaw and horror-struck eyes, obsessively rolling the sheet between her fingers. Then suddenly, just as I was about to withdraw, she puckered her lips and, curling her arm around my neck, pulled my face towards hers. It was our last living embrace." He paused and peeped at my face, as if he were checking upon the effectiveness of his words, to see whether a few more touches were required to bring tears to my eyes – which, as it happens, were dry.

'"She died the following Wednesday," he continued, "having lapsed into a coma during the weekend. As usual, I took our daughter to see her after school. I can still hear her anguished yelp as she leant over the bed, 'Look at Mummy's hands!'

'"A nurse told us that her circulation was beginning to break down. In desperation, my little girl grabbed her mother's hands and began to rub them between her own. Sure enough, the purple blotches disappeared, and their proper pigment was restored. But they wouldn't stay pink for long. So she rubbed them again and refused to stop. My wife, of course, was completely oblivious to this life-and-death struggle. Her eyes were open, but they saw nothing. I couldn't let it continue. 'Come,' I said, gently pulling my daughter away, 'let's go to the cafeteria – I'll buy you a Coke.' When we returned, a few minutes later, the curtains were drawn around my wife's bed." He looked at me again. This time, I was weeping. I couldn't swear to it, but it seemed to me that there was a guilty smirk on his face.'

The Israeli downs her second vodka and orders a third.

'After dinner, we retired to the hotel terrace,' she continues. 'We could see the outlines of the pyramids in the distance, but alas, their spell was broken by a Las Vegas cabaret. The Dreamgirls, shapely women clad only in black waistcoats and fishnet tights, were dancing energetically to recordings such as "Strangers in the Night" and songs from *Cabaret*. Egypt was put to flight by the razzmatazz, and so were we.

'I awoke in the early hours to see a huge moon, apparently balanced on the apex of the largest pyramid, like the all-seeing eye on the reverse of a dollar bill. I arose like a sleepwalker, pulled on a T-shirt and walked out onto the balcony. The Englishman was already there – perhaps he never went to bed – also moonstruck. The air was warm and full of strange noises – indefinable sounds, among which I recognized only the call of the faithful to prayer, the crowing of cocks, the barking of dogs. "This is magic," I said. The Englishman moved towards me, so that only the low glass partition separated us. "I'd call it gorgeous," he said. His body seemed tense, expectant; his eyes were full of longing. Of course, I knew what he wanted me to do. He wanted me to hook him with my arm, just as his dying wife had done, and kiss him on the mouth. But I could not do it. I am a married woman. At the same time, I was naked beneath my T-shirt and could feel the intimate caresses of the pungent air. If only the Englishman had summoned up the courage and made *aliya* to my balcony, I would have succumbed to his embrace and the night. Instead, we stood silently for an hour or more, not even touching, while the descending moon rolled down the side of the pyramid like a silver ball.

'A few hours later, we had breakfast together. He told me that he had just experienced a terrible nightmare. He had seen Michael Holroyd wearing a black robe like a burnous. In his hand, he held a bloody butcher's knife.

"What can it mean?" he asked. I said that first I would have to know this Michael Holroyd. He said that he was a famous British biographer. "Beats me," I said. Can you understand it, Mr Wassef?'

Well, I am only the Egyptian, not Joseph the soothsayer, but even so, I think I can make sense of it. The Englishman feels guilty, as well he might. He sees himself as a biographer, i.e., a character assassin. And, like the figure in his dream, who received a fortune for his biography of George Bernard Shaw, he hopes to profit from his act of betrayal. Who is the Englishman betraying? His late wife, naturally. He probably doesn't even realize it himself, except in the realm of dreams, but that's what he is doing. He kids himself that he is a suffering soul, but deep down he knows that he is a calculating bastard. Why, even I would think twice about using the death of my wife as an aid to seducing another woman. 'Beats me, too,' I say.

'Mr Wassef,' says the Israeli, a little tipsily, 'may I ask you another question?'

'Be my guest,' I say.

'We try so hard,' she says. 'We don't expect you to love us, but can't you at least make the effort to like us?'

I am not nicknamed El Sayed for nothing. The Englishman may have hesitated at the first hurdle, but tonight I am ready to o'erleap the Suez Canal. 'Shall we take a stroll?' I say.

We are walking in the hotel garden. 'Oh, Mr Wassef,' giggles the Israeli, linking her arm in mine, 'I feel a little light-headed.' I stop, look at her with all the sincerity I can muster and, as if overwhelmed by the night-scented jasmine, embrace her. At first, her body registers surprise, then it slowly relaxes, and her lips part, allowing my tongue the access it desires. Now is the moment of abandonment, the time to speak freely: 'Let's go up to your room,' I say *sotto voce*.

'You must forgive the mess, Mr Wassef,' she says.

'My name is Yonnan,' I say.

'Yonnan,' she echoes, 'Yonnan, Yonnan,' again and again, as though trying to memorize a difficult foreign word. She strokes my cheek. 'Please do not jump to any false conclusions, Yonnan,' she says. 'I have never done anything like this before; I have always been a faithful wife.' She begins to tell me about her marriage, her husband's career, her children and her own job at the university. A familiar litany! It seems that Israeli women are no different from all other women. Counterfeit a little respect, and they are yours!

'For two thousand years or more, Jews everywhere recited the prayer "Next Year in Jersualem",' she says, while unbuttoning her blouse. 'Now that seed has come to fruition; we inhabit the city. But it is an earthly city, built not of dreams but of limestone. Do not misunderstand me, Mr Wassef; I think the creation of our state is little short of miraculous. Even so, it is not quite what we had in mind. We are still not at peace with ourselves, let alone our neighbours.' She begins to unclasp her brassière.

'My husband is a good man,' she continues 'albeit, I regret to say, with a blind spot towards the Arabs, and our marriage is a strong one. But it is not quite what I had in mind for myself. I adore my two children. Never doubt that. Should you ever threaten them, Mr Wassef, I would shoot you without hesitation. Yet even they are not quite what I had in mind. I hate myself for it, but if their school reports are less than excellent, if their conversation falls short of sparkling, I am disappointed. Yes, as each day starts with the morning dew, so does disappointment cling to my life. Why am I opening my soul to you, Mr Wassef? Is their something in your character that draws me out? You are handsome and you are charming, but I am a grown woman – a feminist, even – who harbours no secret desire for the Sheikh of Araby.'

Pretending to listen, I walk across the room – it is indeed in a state, underwear and other intimate apparel littering the floor, as though her suitcase were a seed pod that had ripened and burst asunder – and lift a mango from the fruit bowl. Picking up the knife, I cut myself a slice. 'Would you rather that I went?' I enquire.

Never before has anyone given themselves to me so completely, so enthusiastically. The lady with the laptop writhes beneath me, groans, digs her nails into my back, squeals, sweats, and finally, flinging her arms out wide, calls upon her god to witness her transports of delight. Afterwards she says, 'Please don't think badly of me.'

I sigh and kiss her on the breast. 'You were magnificent,' I say.

'I don't mean as a lover,' she says, 'I mean as a woman.'

So I flatter her and cajole her and generally tell her what she wants to hear. However, I do not tell her what she needs to know, which is that my condom, unable to withstand the ferocious passion of an uncircumcised female, has ruptured *in medias res*.

'You are mocking me,' says the Israeli.

'No,' I lie, 'I am smiling because I am happy.' Actually, I am relishing the delicious irony of this bluestocking returning from a conference on population control with a bellyful of Egyptian sperm. I can already hear Shafik's guffaw as I recount the details of my latest conquest.

AND THEN, as the imam said they would, the heavens open. For a few days, we are all Venetians as the monsoon turns our streets into rivers. Further to the south, it is much worse. Floods wash away some sleepers, which causes a train to derail. This, in turn, crashes into an oil depot, which ignites and destroys a village called Dronka. 'It was like winds of fire coming down the mountain,' says a survivor. Another survivor is a baby boy found floating, like Moses, on a makeshift raft of straw. Recuperating in hospital, Naguib Mahfouz condemns the fanatics who put him there: 'I pray to God to make the police victorious over terrorism and to purify Egypt from this evil.' Shafik assures me that he is expected to make a full recovery. In return, I tell Shafik about my over-enthusiastic coupling with the Israeli. However, his applause does not provide me with the anticipated satisfaction. On the contrary, I feel unclean. Nor can I stop thinking about the Israeli. I keep seeing her troubled face and hearing the words, 'Please don't think badly of me.' I wonder whether she really is pregnant. Soon I have become as single-minded as the Englishman; everything reminds me of the Israeli, even my own wife. As a result, I resolve to treat her more kindly.

'Why don't you ever empty your pockets?' she grumbles,

handing me some scraps of paper gleaned from soiled trousers destined for the laundry. 'Thank you, my dear,' I reply, rather than curse her for her nosiness, and am rewarded with the rediscovery of my lover's e-mail address. I use it as soon as I arrive at the office, concocting a message with the aid of a newly acquired Hebrew dictionary. *Rachel, ani ohev otach.* Rachel, I love you.

Why am I doing this? What do I hope to gain? All I know is that this is only the beginning, and that the end is far, far away.

At night, I go out and watch the sky. The rain has cleared the air, and the stars seem to shine with a renewed vigour. Somewhere, amid that glorious firmament, is the satellite which transmits my daily mantra, my hope for the future. I search the heavens for that molecular green light. It is there, of that I am certain, even though I have yet to see it.

For Pamela

Smart-Alecks

I'M A SMART-ALECK JEW-BOY from the suburbs, grammar-school educated, but no academic. Unwilling to take my cues from books, but blessed with a silver tongue, I became an *improvisatore*, a master of the spontaneous gesture, always on the lookout for the lucky break that would transform my life. In the meantime, having no alternative, I worked in the family business. Even so, I continued to regard myself as a free agent, not quite an outlaw; the Zeitgeist Kid. The spirit of the age being *laissez-faire*, no questions asked.

None the less I thought it prudent to keep quiet about my origins in the company of certain folk. Do you really think that the lovely Fiona Bullfinch would have been seen dead with me if she had an inkling that my dad was the purveyor of kosher cuts to the orthodox fishwives of Mill Hill? I can just picture her standing outside Maxie's Meat Empire on the Broadway, her cultured eyes popping from her head at the sight of those small-town vulgarians – with their *shtetl* ways, their padded shoulders, and their designer *sheitels* – squabbling with pater over the price of *kishkas*.

'How quaint,' she would say, before being overcome by homesickness for Knightsbridge. It was a feeling I understood, for I too had metropolitan longings. True, my family were regarded as aristocracy in Mill Hill, father being known as the Emperor Max, but no one – not even someone as credulous as Miss Bullfinch – could possibly have mistaken him for the rightful heir to the Habsburg throne. It was also true that I was spoken of as the Crown Prince, Alexander the Great, but that was a strictly local honorific; my goal was to be King of the City.

I MET FIONA through my friend Pinkie, who pursued a respectable career in Hatton Garden, and ran a less reputable enterprise from the apartment we shared in Mayfair. Given the unsuitability of most of my post-adolescent friendships, the idea of establishing a bachelor pad with Pinkie was welcomed by my parents. Pinkie, they thought, had his head screwed on. Little did they suspect that my immaculate flatmate was a fence for the upper classes, a latter-day court Jew; his particular speciality being drug-dependent debs and chinless scions with gambling debts, who purloined mummy's jewels and relied upon Pinkie's connections for their readies. They felt comfortable dealing with Pinkie because they trusted him, and because they knew they were hardly likely to encounter him at a social occasion.

'That's what I appreciate about you Shylocks,' explained one nobleman, 'you really are only interested in money.' As it happens, m'lord, Pinkie's antecedents were not Venetians, but came from Warsaw via Antwerp, where they traded in industrial diamonds and founded the company their errant descendant was destined to control when old man Straus retired. On account of these prospects Pinkie was regarded as *filet mignon* by the matchmakers of Mill Hill. But neither he nor I (who was also prime *bifteck*) wanted to marry a Millie, any more than we wished to step into the tight-fitting shoes of our fathers. We fled the suffocating embrace of a suburban marriage with relative ease; cutting the economic umbilicus was another matter.

Anyway, Fiona showed up one Sunday with a plastic bag from Harrod's which, I later discovered, contained her older sister's tiara.

'Hey,' she said.

'Hey,' I said.

'Where's Pinkie?' she enquired.

'In Hatton Garden,' I replied, 'at the shop.'

She wrinkled her nose, as if the very word *shop* were a trifle gamey. So when she eventually asked me if I had an occupation I considered it unnecessarily frank to reveal that while I had one foot planted in Mayfair, the other remained firmly rooted in Mill Hill. I had a vision of myself in my bleached hat and bloodstained coat and told a white lie, 'I'm a doctor, well, a surgeon actually.'

'Wow,' she said, impressed but not sufficiently interested to pursue the matter. In many people the absence of a measurable personality would be regarded as a social hindrance, but in Fiona's case it merely highlighted her physical charms, just as the dull setting of her sister's treasured heirloom made the diamonds seem all the more magnificent.

The better educated will know what happened to the daughter of King Midas after he absentmindedly touched her. Well, Fiona could have been her sister. Her tresses were blonde, her grey irises speckled with golden flecks. Her thighs and shapely calves appeared gold-plated, thanks to her glittering stockings. Her face glowed. If Cleopatra bathed in milk, Fiona obviously showered in honey. Her matching dress was the colour of cling peaches. She was high and flirty. Instead of the Sunday roast she had presumably satisfied her appetite with a less traditional line or two. I looked at my watch. Pinkie would not be back for hours. I concluded that there was plenty of time for some love in the afternoon.

'It's not Buckingham Palace,' I said, 'but it beats the dentist's waiting room. At least you can listen to some music till Pinkie shows up.'

Fiona made herself at home, while I put on The Doors. 'Five to one, baby, one in five,' growled the late Jim Morrison, 'no one here gets out alive.'

'That's creepy,' said Fiona.

'But true,' I replied. By then Morrison was in religious mode. 'Now you get yours, baby,' he promised, 'I'll get mine.' It was a philosophy I heartily endorsed, both in theory and in practice.

I have a number of routines for these occasions, most relying on verbal virtuosity or intellectual dexterity. Since neither was appropriate in this case I decided to simply charm the pants off Fiona. I may not have any academic qualifications to boast of, but if there were a University of Charm I'd have graduated *summa cum laude*. It helps that I'm a handsome fellow with a bit of muscle, needless to say. If you want a fully paid-up member of the intellectual élite, a real Arthur Miller type, you should meet my cousin, Noah, another refugee from Mill Hill. I don't know why I bother with Noah, we've nothing in common, except that we grew up together, and he's the last link with my old life. Nor, to be honest, do I know why he bothers with me; yet Noah was the only one of my family who didn't sit *shiva* for me when the sky fell in. He'll be here in a few minutes, if you're interested, when the visitors are admitted.

So I sat down beside Fiona on the sofa and told her she reminded me of Shirley Eaton in *Goldfinger*. I thought that might be a more congenial reference than Greek mythology, but she still hadn't a clue who I was talking about. To help her out I pictured the famous scene when Bond finds her prone on the duvet.

'Dead?' asked Fiona.

'Dead as mutton,' I replied, 'and dressed only in gold paint.' To make things even clearer my hands described the route of the brush on Shirley's stand-in.

'Ah,' said Fiona, getting the point at last.

When I returned from the bathroom kitted out with a state-of-the-art condom Fiona said, 'Sorry, it's against my religion.'

'What's the alternative?' I enquired.

'There are ways, stupid,' the butt-naked aristocrat replied, 'otherwise the whole world would be overrun by Catholics.'

I didn't demur and entered Indo-China in the manner prescribed by *Il Papa*.

'God, Alex,' cried Fiona, climaxing like the Flying Scotsman, 'you're the tops.' If my major was Charm, I own up to a distinguished minor in Fucking. 'Where did you learn to make love like that?' my new friend asked, having recovered from her post-coital swoon.

I could hardly joke, as I often did, 'My business is carnal knowledge,' so I said, 'At medical school.'

'What,' she said, 'with the nurses?'

'Certainly,' I replied, 'but better yet were female cadavers. The trick was to make them come.'

'You could do that?' gasped Fiona.

'If you were good enough,' I replied.

'Oh, Alex,' said the silly girl, 'you can fuck me till I die.'

I was still killing her when Pinkie turned up, accompanied by a dapper gent, with a touch too much melanin to be a proper toff. As it happened Wasim hailed from Lahore though, like us, he was now an accredited denizen of Mayfair. He was also the owner of the Kensington Safe Deposit Company, where Pinkie stashed his loot between owners. 'Wasim has joined me because he needs some advice, some financial advice,' explained Pinkie.

Wasim bowed toward Fiona. 'Your loveliness has enabled me to forget my troubles for a few moments,' he said, 'which puts me in your debt. If I can ever repay you do not hesitate to seek me out. I promise not to flee from you as I do my other creditors.' I recognized a fellow graduate, like me Wasim spread straight from the fridge, a proper *shmoozer* as mother would say. When he finally departed it was as the fawning custodian of Fiona's contraband. Fiona, for her part, left doubly satisfied, overflowing with Alex's seminal fluid, and clutching a bagful of Pinkie's used banknotes.

Before long I too was in need of financial advice from Pinkie. I could just about manage a Mayfair address on the wage my father paid, but dating Fiona, who would only patronize the most fashionable eateries, was putting me in the red. Pinkie, bless him, agreed to make me an interest-free loan. Believe me, after that it came as quite a deliverance when Fiona confessed that I was not her only beau, that she was also seeing a fellow who claimed to be the Anastasia of Iraq. Her relief when she realized that I was not jealous was actually quite touching.

'You really don't mind,' she exclaimed, 'you are prepared to carry on just as we are?'

'Certainly,' I replied, 'it is already forgotten.' As if I could be hurt by a woman with the emotional bite of Pavlov's dog!

'Oh, Alex,' cried Fiona, 'you are so classy.'

How wrong she was; to have class implies substance, and I was but a *luftmensh*, a man of air, fully aware that one day my bubble would burst. I suppose that's why I always used to envy Noah. He seemed to have such gravitas, such firm foundations; a pretty wife, a lectureship at the University of St Albans, a reputation, even an oeuvre. And finally, to crown it all, the cutest daughter you ever saw. He was a lucky man, or so I thought. Now only Job would envy him.

'YOU LOOK THIN, Noah,' I say as he enters the Visitors' Room, hand in hand with his daughter, 'you can't afford to lose any more weight.'

'You sound like my late mother,' he replies glumly.

I turn my attention to his daughter. 'Hello, doll,' I say, kissing her on the cheek, 'lovely to see you.' Then I observe the inch-long cicatrice on her forehead.

'My poor Rosie,' I say, 'such a nasty scar. Whatever happened? You look like someone tried to scalp you.'

'She had an accident, a foolish accident,' replies Noah, 'in Egypt.'

'Oh yes,' I say, 'thanks for the postcard.' I invite my guests to be seated. 'This is my Egypt,' I say, 'we have hard taskmasters, harder even than the chairs. They expect us to make bricks without straw.'

As we relax Noah suddenly notices my broken nose. 'Good heavens, Alexander,' he cries, 'how did you come by that?'

'Also an accident,' I reply, 'I slipped on a bar of soap in the shower.' He knows the truth, of course, that informers rank with child molesters on this side of the prison wall. 'Entertain me,' I say, 'tell me what the pair of you have been doing since you got back from the land of the pharoahs.'

'Daddy took me to hear a lecture by Professor Frankfurter at London University,' volunteers Rosie.

'Trust your dad!' I exclaim. 'Most other fathers would treat their daughters to a Walt Disney cartoon or a show like *Cats*. But that's far too common for my cousin, eh, Mr Smarty-Pants?' I'm gratified by Rosie's giggles. 'This one has to *schlep* his thirteen-year-old to hear a superannuated fart talk about . . . Enlighten me, Noah, give me some gems to share with my cell-mate.' I can see that I have rubbed salt in open wounds.

'Sticks and stones, Alex,' says Noah. 'Are you really of the opinion that I should allow Rosie to become yet another passive consumer? Am I wrong to value Belmont over Brent Cross, to want her to study History and English rather than Shopping? Is it an abuse of power to let her know that there

70

is more to life than getting and spending?' The sanctimonious prig! When we were teenagers Noah developed a stammer. If I'm a smart-aleck, he's always been too clever by half, and I felt genuine regret when the impediment vanished as suddenly as it had come. As the newly unfettered words poured forth I had to suppress an urge to punch him on the nose. The desire has returned, with a vengeance. 'I stand corrected,' I say, clenching my fists. But I do not land the blow; instead I resolve to wound him with words. 'Rosie,' I say, 'please tell Alex what you learned from Professor Frankfurter.'

Rosie blushes, highlighting the snow-white hyphen on her forehead. 'That modern Jewish history is not all tragedy,' she says, 'that there are great achievements too.'

'It took him a whole hour to say that?' I ask.

'I didn't hear it all,' confesses Rosie, 'I fell asleep.'

I turn to Noah in triumph. 'Perhaps you would be good enough to fill in the gaps,' I say.

'I also didn't take it all in,' he replies.

'By God,' I cry, 'it must have been the most boring lecture in history.'

'On the contrary,' replies Noah, 'it began with a dramatic tour de force. The eminent professor emeritus, his cosmopolitan voice hardly more than a mesmeric whisper, begged us – his audience – to suspend our disbelief, to conceive of a world in which the Holocaust never occurred. He was not asking anyone to deny that six million died, God forbid, but to envision a contemporary mittel-Europe still teeming with Jewish life. Our erudite guide led us into that imaginary commonwealth, where he singled out the protean achievements of that lost generation, thanks to which the Nobel

Prize had effectively become a local monopoly. Then, incongruously, he began to talk about Essex, Jewish Essex, to be precise; meaning, presumably, Chingford and Ilford. Why did the professor bring these places to mind? Did he mean to contrast them with Vienna, Prague, and Lvov, to satirize them as the epitome of Anglo-Jewish culture? But by then I was no longer listening. Two short syllables – *s-x* – that's all it took to make me feel like Proust as he bit into the famous tea-stained madeleine. The professor might have quickened the dead, but he had lost me; I was elsewhere, walking in a garden.

'At least it looked like a garden full of willows and roses, but the illusion was spoiled by a tall chimney with a greasy quiff of black smoke. I entered the crematorium, said my wife's name, and waited while the receptionist found the cardboard box, with the urn inside, which I placed on the back seat of the car. I didn't feel it proper to leave it there when I reached home, so I carried it in with me, and sat the thing on the sofa. Rosie flounced in from school later that afternoon. She saw the box at once. 'What's that?' she enquired. 'Not *what*,' I replied, 'but *who*.' We took Charity back to Essex, scattered her ashes there, in the village that had become her once and future home. It was the finale of her ghastly *via dolorosa*.' He smiles at his daughter. 'That's why I can't tell you what else the professor said. Perhaps if I had listened more intently I would have learned how to conjure up a world without cancer, a world without Ward No. 11 at its nether end, a world that still embraced my wife.'

•

I SHUDDER AS I remember Charity's penultimate station, Ward No. 11, the cancer ward. At least there is some logic, some justice if you like, in my present incarceration; there was crime and there is punishment. But what had Charity ever done to earn her place on death row? Good deeds were her daily bread. She was the deputy head of a special school on the outskirts of Watford which assessed children with behavioural and learning difficulties, kids that ordinary comprehensives couldn't handle. After her death the head-masters of those schools wrote Noah such heartfelt tributes that I suspected they were all half in love with her. Why not? I fancied her myself, though she wouldn't have touched a sociopathic Thatcherite like me with a bargepole. But a committed headmaster was different; maybe she did recip-rocate, in word or even deed, but that is hardly a capital offence, hardly sufficient to bring down upon her mortal flesh the torments of the dammed.

She was only forty-six, though by the time she was admitted to Ward No. 11 you'd never have guessed. Not that she cared what she looked like by then. Vanity, dignity, personality; all gnawed away by the flesh-eating pain. Her silk scarves were neatly folded on the bedside table, leaving her bald pate uncovered on the pillow. Her long hair had fallen out in midwinter, all at once, ten days after the first course of chemotherapy, when they were already hoping that she might be spared. Noah recalled finding it in the bathroom, stuffed into a straw basket, as though it were the topknot of a freshly guillotined head. It might just as well have been.

'Any change?' I asked, as if I couldn't see. 'Not for the better,' replied Noah. In those days, incredible as it may seem, there was still talk of a cure. Now we are wiser, know that the prescription delivered by the world-famous cancer expert in his book-lined office was a beautiful *idea*, a platonic cure. He was like an old master who sketched out a work of genius, and then deployed his menials to execute it in his studio where, despite everyone's best intentions, it became a shadow of its former self. Likewise, the great oncologist's panacea was betrayed by human frailty – Charity's and the doctors' alike – not to mention the internal politics of hospital life.

I noticed that the woman in the bed opposite looked even worse than Charity. Moments later, as I observed the curtains being closed around her bed, I understood why. Through a gap in the drapes I watched a couple of nurses brush her hair, straighten the sheets, and generally prepare the late resident for her final despairing visitors. They were chatting, probably about the approaching weekend. Suddenly their work and their conversation was interrupted by a Munch-like scream. They sought its source, and lit not on a heartbroken spouse but upon another nurse, tiptoe on a chair, pointing in horror towards the open door, left ajar to encourage the circulation of summer air. It had incidentally facilitated the entry of a fledgeling blackbird.

'Why are you making that racket?' asked a nurse, who bore an anatomical resemblance to the housemaid in the Tom and Jerry cartoons.

'It's only a bird, not a mouse.'

'I'm terrified of the things,' wailed the elevated nurse, 'please get rid of it.'

The other nurse sniggered and, cupping her hands, bent to gather up the misguided chick. Sensing the approaching wings of a predator it sensibly hopped away, seeking sanctuary beneath the nearest bed. The fat nurse dropped to her knees and, displaying a meaty rump, attempted to coax the bird out of its hiding place. 'Come on, baby,' she whispered, 'come to mummy.' Naturally the terrified creature was not amenable to cajolery and tottered off on its yellow stilts, carefully hugging the perimeter of the ward. The nurse continued the pursuit on all fours, accompanied now by all her colleagues, save for the one on the chair, and the couple grooming the deceased who were, none the less, enjoying the spectacle. And why not? If death can squat in Arcadia, why shouldn't *joie de vivre* be permitted a foothold in oblivion's antechamber?

The bird led them a merry chase, but was finally – inevitably – cornered beneath the bed of the lately departed by the posse of nurses. They all knelt, intent upon securing the space between the mattress and the floor, apparently indifferent to the dead weight above them. The corpse remained equally unconcerned as the daughters of Papageno cooed under its cot. The fugitive refused to budge, obviously mistaking the sisters of mercy for angels of death. This pantomime continued until the avian impressionists were temporarily silenced by yet another unearthly shriek. 'It's a bloody cabaret,' laughed one of the nurses, 'no sooner do we trap one than a second bird shows up in the ward.' Urged on by their fat-assed leader they re-entered the lower depths, and resumed their twittering.

The bereaved husband stared at the row of backsides in silent astonishment. Perhaps he thought he was watching some last mark of respect to his wife, a Muslim-style requiem, a time-honoured ritual of farewell peculiar to Ward No. 11. If so he was definitively disabused when the in-house Diana arose triumphantly with the petrified bird in her grasp. Her colleagues also stood, looking like a demented chorus-line. Seeing at once the dead woman's erstwhile partner they attempted to do to their giggles what Richard III did to his nephews in the Tower. Unlike the princes the giggles refused to die. 'Have you no respect?' cried the poor man, struggling to retain control of his emotions. I confess that I was laughing too, and I'm willing to swear that Noah smiled.

If the world is divided between those who are trapped in Ward No. 11 and those who are free to come and go, then that flicker of joviality indicated that Noah, for all his vicarious suffering, was still on our side. At the same time Charity's predicament demonstrated that the boundaries were far from fixed, and that even the most open-hearted and optimistic among us were not secure. One minute we are calmly chewing the cud with the rest of the herd, the next our flesh is on display in the window of Maxie's Meat Empire. *C'est la vie*.

But the *comédie larmoyante* was not quite *finito*. With a spine-tingling howl the widower flung himself on the bier. 'Now that's what you call grief,' said Noah admiringly. Meanwhile the abashed nurses opened the window and watched the fledgeling ascend to the heavens, as if it were the dead woman's absconding soul.

'THE IRONY IS that Professor Frankfurter wasn't talking about Essex at all,' says Noah, sheepishly breaking the silence. 'It was all a misunderstanding; my fault, I forgot about his thick accent. You see, he was discussing ethics.' Noah guffaws. '*Ethics* not *Essex!*'

'Ethics, shmethics,' I say, 'that's what people like the professor want you to think they care about. Don't you believe a word of it. Take that crap about a world full of renevant Jews. That's the last thing Frankfurter really wants. He knows that if the six million returned en masse he'd lose his *raison d'être* and his precious moral superiority at a stroke. The noble professor may rail against the Nazis and their ilk, but that enmity is as nothing compared to the venom he reserves for the real villains; his competitors. It's all vanity, cousin, vanity of vanities. You look sceptical. But I have the proofs, if you'd care to lend an ear.' Rosie yawns. I pat her head, then turn toward her father.

'A couple of years ago a friend of mine – an ex-friend of mine, I should say – became the literary editor of the *Jewish Voice*. Being as keen as mustard he wanted to get big names to write for him, so naturally he invited Frankfurter to be a contributor. The intellectual leviathan agreed, on condition the supplicant first repaired an earlier slight committed by the paper. Accordingly when the professor's next master-piece was published the literary editor commissioned a review from a well-known admirer. By happy coincidence a freelance photographer turned up at his office simul-taneously, and mentioned that the professor was due to sit for him on the morrow. 'Would you like to see some prints?' he enquired. 'Certainly,' replied the literary editor. He kept his part of the bargain, publishing a flattering review, as well as a token photograph of the sagacious scribe.

'A few weeks later he was invited to hear the pedagogue *extraordinaire* give a public lecture at Trinity College, Cambridge. He made the journey weighed down with a bag full of books. After the oration the select audience retired to a bar in a corner of the quadrangle where the literary editor, having insinuated himself among the professor's entourage, displayed his wares, in the hope that one of the tomes would catch the great man's fancy. The professor was as nice as pie, but said there was a minor problem, which he preferred to discuss in private. So the pair strolled together across the greensward in the direction of the dining hall. Once they were out of earshot the professor's mood underwent an alarming transformation. He began to wag his finger, as though chastizing a *dummkopf*, whilst shouting, yes shouting, 'It was not good enough! It was not good enough!' True the review wasn't profound, thought the shocked literary editor, but at least it called him a genius. What more did he want? 'I spent the entire morning with the photographer you sent,' complained the professor, making a frame out of his thumb and first finger, 'and all you could do was print a picture the size of postage stamp. I tell you, sir, it's not good enough!'

'I know just how the prof felt. I was also pissed off when the *Jewish Voice* published my mugshot, admittedly for the opposite reason. It was too bloody big!'

'Anecdotal evidence,' says Noah. 'I'd like to hear the other side of the story before I pass judgement. Suppose the photographer disturbed some private reverie, turned out to be another "Man from Porlock".'

I sit on my hands.

'Why is it so hard to accept that Frankfurter's a phony?' I say. 'I may not have the brains of the men you admire, Noah, but at least I'm no hypocrite. I don't pretend to be other than I am; a cocksure crook who got caught with his fingers in the cookie jar.'

BUT I ALWAYS had style – my credo being *le style est l'homme même* – which is why I got invited to parties by Pinkie's clients and he didn't. It was at a housewarming hosted by a Pre-Raphaelite beauty with post-modern cravings that I first set eyes on the pretender to the throne of Iraq. Fiona was bisected by an equatorial dress that barely covered the tropics; her despot manqué sported a navy blazer, neatly pressed slacks, and soft leather moccasins. He looked natty enough, but the real art was to be found in the details, those carefully chosen accessories which quietly spelled out *royalty*; the silk shirt with the crowned monogram, the crested cuff links, the military tie, the heroic decoration in the buttonhole. And yet I was not fooled for a moment; this was no princeling, but merely an actor who had raided the props cupboard. Not quite Cary Grant, more the Tony Curtis impersonation in *Some Like it Hot*. I was being cuckolded by a conman; another bullshit artist, with as much blue blood as me. For all I knew he wasn't even an Iraqi. He was clearly an Arab of some sort, but that was as much as I was prepared to concede.

The Sheik of Araby glanced round and, spotting me, blew through the crowded room like a simoom. I stood my ground, ready to pay for my *lèse-majesté*. But this off-the-peg King Hussein was amity personified. 'Our encounter is kismet,' he announced, offering me his hand. 'Surely we are destined to be *confrères*, if not blood brothers. How else to describe men who share the favours of a woman, whose seed has mingled in her womb? Tell me all about yourself. I understand that you are a doctor. Is that right?'

'More a surgeon,' I replied modestly.

'Brilliant,' he said, 'my cousin, Saddam, is a sawbones at the Middlesex. Perhaps you know of him?'

'Afraid not,' I replied, 'I work with Magda Yacoub at the Harefield.'

'What a coincidence,' he exclaimed, 'another cousin, Walid, is Sir Magda's right-hand man. As a matter of fact, I have been invited to hear Sir Magda sing in his church choir on Sunday morning. Will you be there too?'

'Alas, no,' I said, 'I shall be on duty this weekend.'

'What a pity,' he said, 'we could have gone together. Compared notes on Fiona. And maybe had lunch at Sir Magda's favourite pub. Remind me of its name.'

I knew he was bluffing, so I made one up. 'The Saracen's Head,' I said.

'Of course,' he replied, 'how could I forget something like that?'

I took my opportunity to turn the tables. 'Is it really true that you are the heir presumptive to the Iraqi throne?' I asked. 'If so I'd be fascinated to learn how you survived the bloodbath of '58. I was under the impression that the entire royal family was butchered.'

The phoney prince laughed. 'Touché,' he said. 'It is time we stopped this charade. I am Prince Bashir like you are a medical man. Bashir, yes; Prince, hardly. We are both –

how shall I put it? – chameleons. We live off our wits, unlike these pampered fops, who care only for their pleasures. Fiona believes our cock-and-bull stories, not because she is completely stupid, but because she lacks sufficient interest in other people to bother whether they're telling her the truth or not. I have studied the English and have become convinced that this lack of curiosity is the defining characteristic of their aristocracy. You, *au contraire*, are a sharp fellow. Just now, when I felt your eyes upon me, I knew at once that you had seen through my façade. You probably have even guessed that I am not an Iraqi. I'm sure you recognize a Maronite from East Beirut when you see one. I doubt Fiona even knows there are Christian Arabs; as far as she is concerned, an Arab is an Arab. Why, I'll wager she doesn't even suspect that you're a Jew.'

He raised his hand. 'Please, my friend, don't insult me by denying it.' There was an implied threat in the words which led me to believe that my new chum Bashir didn't take insults lying down.

'Why should I deny it?' I said. 'Of course I'm a Jew.'

'Excellent,' he said. 'I have no animus. I deal with Jews all the time. So when Fiona described Pinkie – not very flatteringly, I should add – I thought, Here is a man I can do business with. Perhaps you would be good enough to effect an introduction in the near future? It may surprise you to learn that, back home, most of my closest associates are Israelis. Our politicians may be at odds, our religious fanatics at each other's throats, but I am happy to inform you that all is sweetness and light among my fellow tradesmen. We have transcended the endemic hatreds to become genuine internationalists. You have my assurance that there are no borders nowadays in the underworld. What is harvested in the Beka'a on Wednesday is on sale in Tel Aviv or Damascus by Thursday. Like all visionaries we are much misunderstood. We regard ourselves as capitalism's avant-garde, whereas others denounce us as wicked men, despoilers of innocent youth.' He shrugged. 'Profits without honour. We can live with that.'

He smiled at me. 'Now it is your turn to spill the beans, my friend,' he said. 'Indulge my curiosity: if you are not a medical man, what are you?'

'I work in my father's shop in Mill Hill,' I confessed. He wasn't going to be satisfied with that.

'A shop,' he replied, 'what kind of a shop?'

'A kosher butcher,' I said defiantly, 'one of the largest kosher butchers in north-west London.'

'This is another thing we have in common,' laughed the Lebanese drug baron, 'my father was also a butcher. At least that is what his enemies called him, and his enemies were legion. The one with the biggest mouth was Tony Frangipane, who ran his own militia. It seems that Tony's father and my father had a row at one of the big Christian pow-wows. This was not unusual, but big-mouth Tony decided to turn it into a vendetta. He ordered his men to gun down my older brother. So my father took fifty or so Phalangists and surrounded Tony's house. Tony knew better than to surrender. It was like a scene in a movie, you know, *The Gunfight at the OK Corral*. Fortunately we were the Earps. When the shooting was over not only was Tony dead, but also his wife, his daughter, his bodyguards, his servants, and his cattle. If that was how the Phalangists treated their fellow Christians, you can imagine what they did to the Palestinians. I saw it with my own eyes. My father took me with him when they entered Sabra and Shatilla. "We have a strict code of honour," he advised me, "you are forbidden to rape any girls under twelve." He put his arm around my shoulder. "This is Beruit, my son, not Copenhagen. Enjoy yourself." I was a little gentleman that day; I made sure that I ravished no one younger than seventeen. Unfortunately it was not possible to be so fastidious when it came to the executions. After our bloodlust was satisfied, I watched my father and his cronies toast their cheap victory. They were like schoolboys; shooting their guns in the air, and drinking Château Musar from the bottle. But what had these Don Quixotes really achieved? The death of a few hundred unarmed Palestinians? Where was the glory in that? It was a textbook display of bathos, as if the abattoir workers who supply your father were to celebrate their bloody triumph over a multitude of docile cows. No doubt you imagine a more glamorous existence for yourself when you are mincing beef, or quartering a chicken. I was no different, except that I was ready to do more than build castles in the air. My father was a hero to his men, but all I could see was a minor warlord, a suburban Mussolini. I broke his heart when I renounced the succession and quit Beirut. But it was worth it; I worked hard and made my fortune. Now I have come to London to make my name.'

THE THREE OF US approached the Kensington Safe Deposit Company; Pinkie, Bashir, and the Zeitgeist Kid. We were driving a Ford, hired for the day. Bashir had removed the number plates and replaced them with diplomatic forgeries, which gave us an entrée to Embassy Row, conveniently situated a block away from our destination and our destiny. We parked and, wishing the other good luck, split into two parties. Pinkie reached the neo-Egyptian eyesore first, signed the register, and handed his key to a Schwarzenegger clone. They were already descending the spiral staircase as we made our grand entrance. I introduced my companion to the receptionist as Crown Prince Bashir of the royal house of Iraq, and a prospective client. Wasim was summoned. He looked nervous. When he shook our hands his palms were sweaty.

He offered to show us the premises, and led us below stairs, where another Ruritanean hunk carelessly unlocked the iron portal that afforded entry to the vaults. As the door swung upon its hinges Bashir suddenly barged it with his shoulder, throwing the guardian off balance. A further blow to the head with a blunt instrument stunned him sufficiently to allow me to secure him to the radiator. Wasim uttered several expletives, but offered no physical resistance. Hearing the commotion the guard who had been accompanying Pinkie came running, only to stop in his tracks when he found himself face to face with a mustachioed Arab brandishing a revolver. Sensing at once that the wild-eyed son of the desert was prepared to use it, the sensible security man followed Wasim's example and raised his hands, which were duly cuffed by yours truly.

'Is anyone else down here?' demanded Bashir. It was the tail-end of a Monday afternoon, when we knew that the place would be more or less deserted, as well as restocked with the baubles withdrawn for the weekend.

'Just one client,' replied the guard.

'Excellent,' said Bashir, addressing me, 'fetch him.' Pinkie, having more to lose, made a bigger fuss than the custodians, but he too was eventually overcome and bound like the others. For added verisimilitude Wasim was bashed over the crown with the gun butt.

Having secured the basement Bashir revisited the car to collect the tools of our new trade. Returning he closed the Kensington Safe Deposit Company for the night and reappeared with the weeping receptionist in tow. 'Right,' he said, 'let's go to work.'

To open a safe deposit box it is necessary to have a pair of keys: the master key – which we had acquired from Wasim – and the box owner's unique key. Lacking the latter we were forced to use industrial drills and crowbars, which proved to be just as effective. As I worked I hummed the opening lines of a Neil Young song, 'I wanna live, I wanna give, I've been a miner for a heart of gold'. Though, in truth, I felt more like a figment of Scheherezade's imagination than a genuine forty-niner. It was as though the cold store at the rear of Maxie's Meat Empire had undergone a magical transformation, so that the glazed flesh and shiny innards – the ruby-hued mince, the jasperite liver, and the pearly fowl – had actually become the jewels they resembled. As we tore into box after box with increasing frenzy Bashir accidentally cut his hand on a wing of jagged steel. 'Behold,' he cried, displaying his bleeding palm, 'the stigmata. Now our enterprise is truly blessed.' Sure enough it soon became apparent that we were emptying the plumpest cornucopia outside King Tut's tomb.

Bashir's eyes were ablaze like some religious visionary. 'This is fantastic, a dream come true,' he exclaimed, 'a crime *sans pareil.*' I was infected by his passion and penned headlines of my own: ZEITGEIST KID IN BILLION-DOLLAR HEIST. Then it occurred to me that the only famous criminals are the ones who get caught. The essence of the perfect crime is that the perpetrator remains anonymous. This would surely frustrate a born show-off, eager to establish a reputation as the Rembrandt of crime. Did Bashir really possess sufficient self-control to eschew the limelight? Doubts nagged at me. I began to suspect that he secretly intended to leave his signature at the scene. We left little else.

The nightwatchman at Embassy Row actually saluted the pair of us as we drove out in our rented privateer. It took several trips to transfer all the treasure from the car to our Mayfair headquarters. We filled the bathtub with banknotes, and the pantry with packets of cocaine. Rolex and Cartier watches were lined up like tin soldiers on the carpet in the dining room. Gold coins were stacked in columns. There was a lake of diamonds, a hill of rubies, jungle of silverware, and a veritable mountain of gold.

'We'll be millionaires for sure when this lot is shifted,' I burbled.

'Fool,' snapped Bashir, 'you don't begin to understand why I did this, do you?'

He was spot on. Of course I didn't, but then I wasn't entirely sure why I'd become a desperado myself. Obviously I wanted the money, which would free me from my thraldom to the fleshpots of Mill Hill, and finance my independent status. But was that all? Perhaps each destructive blow aimed at the locked boxes had also been a contraction, a labour pain, the birth pangs of a new, improved Alexander; no longer a smart-aleck Jew-boy, but a bona fide member of high society.

'By God,' said Pinkie upon his return from the police station, 'this is what they mean by an embarrassment of riches.' In the course of the following week he began to market some of the more spectacular trinkets, so that we were able to wander through the flat without being blinded by reflected light. One day he returned from his clandestine contacts with a gift for me. 'There was so much gold,' he said, 'almost an excess of the stuff, that I had some of it melted down and fashioned into a calf. I thought you might like to present it to your dad to hang in the shop window. You never know, it might mitigate the shock of your defection.' Pinkie was a good friend who deserved better from me. Needless to say, the ornament was unceremoniously removed when my travel plans were interrupted and I found myself in this bleak penitentiary, rather than the sunkissed shores of the Mediterranean.

I AM IN a bad mood. The last person I want to see is my unctuous cousin. 'Noah, you don't much like me, let alone approve of me,' I say, 'so why are you such a frequent visitor?' Noah opts for inscrutability, offering no word of explanation.

In the meantime an undernourished member of the *lumpenproletariat* (clearly not a subject of the Emperor Max) swings across the room on crutches and lowers himself into a chair opposite a peroxide blonde. Her greeting is inaudible, unlike her visitor's explosive response. 'Don't be a silly cunt,' he yells, 'don't talk like that. It's not the end of the world. The important thing is to get on the good side of your probation officer. Make sure you attend all the meetings. Don't be like me and fuck it up. I blame myself, even though it wasn't entirely my fault. One of the girls had it in for me and told everyone that I'd sold her valium. I swear to God, if it'll help you I'll give the lot up. I love you.' He pauses. 'Why can't you say it back? At least say ditto.' He pauses again. 'Have it your own way. Will you be faithful to me? Once you're out, I mean.' Another pause. 'Tell me the truth,' he demands, 'who is this Mr Green who keeps coming to see you?' At last she says something. 'How do I know?' he cries. 'The screws told me he's here every other day, that's how. Who is he? Bitch! Why won't you put my mind at rest?'

Whereupon my own Mr Green, whose presence I have almost forgotten, decides to reply. 'You're a captive audience,' he says, 'and much cheaper than a shrink.'

'You mean you want the considered advice of a man without higher education,' I say, 'let alone a sense of morality. You must be in dire straits.'

'I just want you to listen,' he says, 'something unexpected has happened.' I deduce, from the absence of his daughter, that it's a case of *cherchez la femme*. 'I'm all ears,' I say, cheering up.

'AS YOU KNOW,' says Noah, 'Rosie insisted upon seeing her mother every day after school. It was hard for me to watch the thirteen-year-old girl lovingly stroke her mother's forehead, and receive barely a glimmer of recognition in return. Somehow Rosie retained her composure and her grace, understood and forgave the maternal negligence. She is a remarkable child, her mother's daughter. Nevertheless I felt it advisable to make contact with her school, if only to ensure that there were no hidden problems with work, or signs of depression that I had missed. I was assured that there were none. "Don't fret, I'll keep an eye on her," said Miss Tiptree, her form teacher, "just in case."

'The trips to Belmont became more commonplace as Charity's condition rapidly deteriorated. At first I sat with Miss Tiptree in the reception area, a public place, then she invited me back to her office, where she often held my hand and wept. I went there straight from Ward No. 11 that terrible day when hope was finally abandoned. Miss Tiptree squeezed my hand as I quoted the consultant's actual words (uttered with tears in her eyes). "In my opinion, Noah, your wife is dying of her disease." She didn't say it, but the unspoken implication was very clear; the sooner the better. Miss Tiptree applied more pressure when I explained that the alternative was not remission (let alone a cure), but increasing agony, turning the natural urge to want Charity to remain alive into a sadistic impulse. However, to wish her dead was impossible. A heartbreaking dilemma, you'll agree, but was I really thinking about it at that moment? No, I was enjoying the sensations aroused by Miss Tiptree's response. Tell me, Alexander, what kind of monster finds gratification in describing such dreadful things?'

'Noah,' I say, 'I fear the pair of us are more alike than either of us would care to admit. We are both magpies, heartlessly taking from others for our own ends. I stole from the anonymous keyholders of the Kensington Safe Deposit

Company, many of whom were gangsters themselves, while you have purloined Charity's suffering. I'm no philosopher, but to my mind your crime is the more heinous of the two.'

'You haven't heard the worst of it,' says Noah.

This is fun. My cousin's visit is turning out much better than anticipated.

'Charity died before the month was out,' he continues. 'Then I took Rosie to Egypt, and I didn't see Miss Tiptree again . . . until three weeks ago. It was a Saturday and I had dropped Rosie at a friend's house, where she had been invited to spend the night. Driving back along Victoria Street I slowed down outside the Rhinoceros Horn to permit a car to pull out of a parking space and, on a whim, because it was a warm evening and I was not eager to return to an empty house, I took it myself.

'Apart from the publican I was undoubtedly the oldest man in the bar. Most of the drinkers seemed to be in their twenties or younger. They were being entertained by a quartet of deluded albinos who thought they were in Memphis, Tennessee. "I'm standing at the crossroads," moaned the singer, "I believe I'm sinking down." Feeling like a living fossil I was about to flee when, to my astonishment, I saw Miss Tiptree march toward the band like a prizefighter, egged on by a gauntlet of hyperventilating sixth formers. Only when she was actually standing on the platform, microphone in hand, did I realize that she intended to sing. Should I go, or should I stay? Curiosity was stronger than embarrassment. I stayed.

'The opening chords were familiar, heralding an anthem from our adolescence. "I'm gonna wait till the midnight hour," she growled, "that's when my love comes tumbling down . . ." I noticed that she looked the part; black tights, short skirt, jumper a couple of sizes too small. What's more she had a voice; husky but sweet, Aretha Franklin with milk and sugar. "I'm gonna wait till the midnight hour, that's when my love begins to shine . . . just you and I . . . nobody around baby . . . just you and I." It's a common delusion, of course, but for a moment I believed that the words were addressed to me. In fact when she did catch sight of me she screamed.

'"Oh, God," she cried, "what must you think of me? The prim school-ma'am who promised to watch over your daughter, completely shit-faced."

'"Let's sit down," I said. She fell into a chair.

'"The seventh gin and tonic," she said, "a huge mistake. I was fine till then." She looked at me and her eyes filled with tears. She touched my cheek. "You look so sad," she said, "if only I could make you smile. At least let me buy you a drink."

I drove her home.

'"Goodnight, petal," she said in the car, outside her flat, then kissed me on the mouth, and ran away. After that I became a regular caller at Miss Tiptree's apartment, though there were no more kisses.

'"Daddy," enquired Rosie, smelling a rat, "you're not going out with Miss Tiptree are you?"

'"No," I replied, 'but would there be a problem if I were?"

'"Of course there would!" she yelled. "Miss Tiptree's my teacher."

'Not withstanding Rosie's proscription I invited Miss

Tiptree out on a proper date. You remember the sort of thing, Alexander. It's the weekend; she gets dressed up, you get dressed up, you pick her up, you hold open the car door. You go to a fancy restaurant where you are shown to a table by Bela Lugosi. Afterwards you pay the bill and, if you are lucky, you get laid. Anyway, Miss Tiptree – Billie – was agreeable, to the first part at any rate. I got dressed up, she got dressed up.

'"What do you think of me?" she said, turning a pirouette on her doorstep. "Don't I look like sex on legs?"

As it happened, she did, but the boast was bravado; Billie was in a state.

'"It's been a week from hell," she announced, as we sped down the motorway towards London. A troubled girl she had befriended, a pupil at Belmont, had repaid her kindness with open allegations of sexual abuse. I told her it reminded me of something that had happened to Charity. At the beginning of her career she had sheltered a runaway instead of turning her in. Her reward had been stolen clothes and a rebuke from the police. It occurred to me that the two women had obvious similarities; above all both had the same ferocious concern for children, especially the wounded ones. The big difference being that Billie was alive and beside me in the car.

'Le Pont de la Tour was very Frenchified, meaning that the waiters all looked like they had stepped out of a Toulouse-Lautrec poster. The *sommelier* held his pad as if he were a *flic* taking evidence as I ordered pink champagne to accompany the hors-d'oeuvres, and one of Randall Grahm's full-bodied reds from Bonny Doon to complement Billie's pan-fried venison and my magret of duck. By way of an aperitif my companion downed a large gin and tonic. The alcohol quickened her appetite and induced mild amnesia, enabling her to concentrate upon the present moment at the expense of Belmont and its attendant traumas. It also loosened her tongue. She raised her glass and said, "You might like to know that there is no one I would rather be with tonight."

'We took our coffee and *digestifs* in the bar where a sweet-faced black man was playing the piano and crooning in a jazzy way. Did it bother him that all the drinkers were ignoring him? All save one, that is. During the next hour Billie drummed her fingers and consumed a further four gins mixed with slimline tonic. Thus fortified she approached the pianist and offered her services as a vocalist. Unfortunately the pianist remained unconvinced that there was much audience demand for 'Mustang Sally'. Billie, however, was persistent. She squatted down beside the stool and pressed the claims of the Wicked Pickett and Van the Man. The pianist continued to maintain that he was prohibited from singing anyone more outré than Elton John. The manageress, seeing his embarrassment, intervened. Billie informed her that she had a beautiful face. Returning to her seat she told the waiter that he too possessed a beautiful face. She tried to stroke it. He recoiled.

'"Where are you from?" she enquired.

'"Poland," he said.

'"Ah," she said, "the Polish also love their drink."

'When we became friends Billie warned me not to invest

anything in her, because she was sure to let me down. And this was clearly what she was trying to do, to disappoint my expectations, to demonstrate her worthlessness, to ruin the evening. But I was not her father, nor would I be her judge. I would not give her the opportunity to turn on me and say, "See, I told you I wasn't worth the candle." Being worthless absolved her of responsibility, removed the fear of failure, and – most importantly – meant that there was no danger of getting hurt. These self-fulfilling prophesies were the landmines she had laid around her heart. Charity's pain had been omnivorous, heedlessly devouring its host. Billie's pain was also self-destructive, but – perversely – it actually increased her value in my eyes, made her allure more persuasive. I determined to circumnavigate all the obstacles and enter the land of milk and honey.

'In order to leave the City it was still necessary to pass through one of the police roadblocks, originally established to trap Republican terrorists. Now that their Molotov cocktails were on ice, the vigilant officials were on the lookout for drivers who preferred to drink the stuff rather than throw it. True, I didn't have springs coming out of the top of my head, like Billie, but there was certainly an excess of intoxicants in my blood. Was this my nemesis? Was I about to be punished for attempted infidelity to a dead spouse with a night in the cells?

'"Where have you been?" asked a policeman as we reached the barrier.

'"To a restaurant," I replied.

'"Have you had anything to drink?" he asked. It was too

dangerous to answer in the affirmative. Who orders a bottle of wine and drinks only two glasses?

'"Alcohol is *verboten*," I said, "I've got cancer."

'I FOLLOWED BILLIE up the stairs to her flat. Once inside she poured herself another gin. She had no tonic, so she added something called Um Bongo. It obviously robbed her of her remaining senses because she suddenly kissed me. Her lips were soft, but the kiss was desperate. I felt as though I were being branded with the letter Q. We subsided to the floor, where a hands-on approach to parent–teacher relations was initiated.

'"Wow," laughed Billie, "I haven't had a snog like this for years."

I unbuttoned her blouse, exposing a white brassière. Charity, being trim, never wore the things. I began to fondle the enclosed breasts. Billie shut her eyes and purred.

'"This is the first working brassière I've encountered in two decades," I remarked, hoping to make light of my trespass. It was a tactical error.

'"I thought you were different," she said, "but you're just like all the rest. Fascinated by my great big tits. If I had the courage I'd chop them off." Weeping she arose, a dishevelled Venus. "Blood and sand," she moaned, "blood and sand." She slumped into the sofa and began to wrestle with her inner demons. These were not invisible abstractions, like Jehovah, but material objects made in the image of Maurice Sendak's Wild Things. They were her scary monsters. She stroked them, hit them, whispered to them, cried over them, threw them across the room. "I must be going mad," she wailed, "I'm talking to puppets."

'"Talk to me instead," I suggested.'

'Was her blouse still undone?' I ask Noah.

'As a matter of fact it was,' he replies.

'So there was still hope?' I ask.

'There was still hope,' he replies.

'Did she talk to you?' I ask.

'She talked,' replies Noah. 'She said she was sick and tired of being strong, of being the life and soul of every gathering. She said she wanted someone to look after her for a change. I offered.

'"It would be a huge mistake," she said, "a huge mistake for both of us. If I don't hurt you, you'll hurt me."

'"I won't," I assured her.

'"It doesn't matter," she said, "I don't intend to give you the opportunity. I'm never never never ever going to let anyone come close to me again." Then she told me about her father, who was a great dad, but drank too much, and about her ex-husband, who ran off with one of her colleagues.

'"Did you love him?" I asked.

'"I loved his bones," she replied, "I still love him. That's my problem."

'"He must have been out of his mind," I said.

'"You're sweet," said Billie. She turned her face towards me and I kissed her. "Tell me," she said, "would you like Charity to come back?"

'"Of course," I said. What else could I say? But to be honest I didn't want anyone other than Billie beside me on the sofa just then. Did this mean that I had subconsciously wished for Charity's death, so that I would be free to pursue other women? President Carter had confessed to being an adulterer in his heart, was I a murderer in mine? Was Charity's blood on my hands? If that was the crime what would be my punishment? I am not a believer, but if I were, my God would be a hanging judge. I shuddered at the thought.

'"Sorry, bad question," said Billie, "let's forget our sorrows and dance."'

'Why do you feel it necessary to turn a simple seduction into a psychodrama?' I say testily. 'I thought Professor Humbugger was swollen-headed, but you take the biscuit; you must have an ego as big as the Ritz. Allow me to remind you that you didn't kill Charity. Cancer did. She died of it in Ward No. 11. Do me a favour, cousin, don't kid yourself; don't use Charity's fate to complicate a simple thing like lust. Is it so hard to admit that Billie Big Tits could see right through you, could see that all you really wanted from her was some animal magic?' We both know that I am right, but Noah would have bitten his tongue off before giving me the satisfaction of confirming it.

'When Billie said, "Let's dance," she wasn't thinking of a conventional *pas de deux*,' he says with a dismissive shrug, 'but of something she called air-dancing, which apparently requires you to lie side-by-side on the floor and wave your arms to the siren sound of heavy metal. As you know, Alexander, I have absolutely no sense of rhythm. An objective observer would have guessed that I was performing a mime, perhaps enacting the ultimate panic of a ship-wrecked sailor. No one, I fear, would have mistaken me for a grieving widower in his mid-forties.'

I can't help myself. The Aswan Dam couldn't have contained my laughter. Poor Noah is mightily offended. 'You are so crude you reduce everything to slapstick,' he complains. 'Even Thanatos is good for a laugh. And Eros, it seems, is simply killing.'

'If you didn't take yourself so seriously,' I say, 'you'd be a lot happier.'

'Like you?' he says cruelly. I can't answer that.

'Meanwhile Rosie's guardian angel was body-surfing,' continues Noah, 'a mile high on Beefeater and Pink Floyd. Our hands met accidently in midair, then our lips with more design. Enboldened I unzipped her skirt. Billie was sporting matching underwear. If I resembled a drowning man, she looked like Esther Williams in a bikini. I slipped my hand beneath the elastic of her panties. Her buttocks, I discovered, were surprisingly cool. "You can lie on top of me," she said.'

'I know what's coming next,' I say, 'or rather what's not coming. You didn't fuck her, did you?'

Noah shakes his head. 'I wish I could tell you it was because I'm too much of a gentleman to take advantage of a soused divorcee,' he says, 'or that I still felt Charity's eternal absence too keenly, but it wouldn't be the truth. My failure had nothing to do with morality or mortality; the sad fact is that I was a chicken shit, too scared to make out with someone I took to be a sexual athlete. The joke is that she wasn't; I found out later that she'd only had two lovers, including her husband. Now she has a third, and it ain't me. A week after our date a long-lost friend turned up unannounced at her front door; a big fellow who mounts a chair as if it were a horse. He's still there, mounting Billie as well as her chairs. "Noah," she said, when we last spoke, "it's happened, my ship has come in."'

He looks like his has sunk. 'What you need,' I say, 'is a brainless tart who'll let you fuck her senseless.' I enjoy Noah's self-loathing too much to ease it with the comforting information that he may well have had a narrow escape. Otherwise I would have told him about Fiona Bullfinch's disturbing news.

SHE TURNED UP unexpectedly a couple of hours ago, looking as beautiful as ever, although conspicuously out of place; an English rose on a dunghill. She handed me a basket of fruit, as if I were a patient and this prison a hospital.

'Fiona,' I said, 'what a pleasant surprise.'

'I've got an even bigger one,' she replied, 'I'm pregnant.'

'Is this a matter for congratulation?' I enquired.

'It depends upon the attitude of the father,' she replied.

'Who is?' I asked.

'You,' she replied.

'How do you know it isn't Bashir?' I asked.

'Because that two-faced swine is serving twenty years,' she replied, 'whereas you'll be out in less than five.'

Suddenly I have become a man with responsibilities, a man whose carefree activities have started to spawn salutary side-effects. 'Have some fruit,' I say to Noah, indicating Fiona's basket. He picks up an apple, then grabs a larger item which he commences to sniff with greedy abandon.

'This is overripe,' he says, as if I care, 'it's got a very

pungent aroma, a mixture of female sweat and sweet deodor-ant. In fact it smells alarmingly like Charity's armpits.'

'What are you saying now,' I snap, 'that your wife has been reincarnated as an Israeli melon?' Has the man who denounces materialism with prophetic zeal finally cracked? Has he found that he needs more to sustain him than an invisible wife? I note with grim satisfaction that the poor bastard takes the melon home with him when he goes.

BETWEEN ONE O'CLOCK and two it was the custom for the owners to leave the shop in the hands of one of the assistants and retire to a back room, where they ate pastrami on rye (which the master butcher insisted upon calling a salt-beef sandwich) and watched the lunchtime news. Full mouth or not my father would frequently abuse the report-ers, particularly when they exposed their antisemitic hearts by making uncomplimentary remarks about Israel. 'Calm down, for God's sake,' I would say, 'you'll give yourself an ulcer.'

On the day my chickens came home to roost we switched on the television a little late and missed the headlines. Instead we were treated to a story about a bunch of hysterical bleeding-hearts, the ones who were blockading the nation's ports in a determined effort to prevent the export of live calves to the vile veal-lovers across the Channel.

'These poor creatures are suffering dreadfully, and will endure even worse when they are eventually imprisoned by the continentals in their infamous crates,' said a woman in green wellies and a headscarf, who could have been Fiona

Bullfinch's granny. 'It is a crime against humanity, every bit as wicked as the Nazi treatment of the Jews.'

'Did you hear that?' screamed my father. 'That bloody woman is only equating the annihilation of millions with the plight of a few cows, who are for the chop anyway. The English have a funny sense of priorities. I'm sure most of them would be more comfortable tucking into their fellow citizens than the beasts of the field.'

He continued to lambast the perverse mores of the *goyim*, but I was no longer listening. I probably wasn't even breathing. In fact it was a miracle I didn't faint as the newsreader informed her viewers that there had been a breakthrough in the hunt for the men who had raided the Kensington Safe Deposit Company. A bloodstain found at the scene had yielded a pair of perfect fingerprints which matched a set already on file at Interpol. Bashir's visage appeared on the screen, sporting a fierce moustache. He was characterized as an international drugs-dealer with terrorist connections, and said to be armed and extremely dangerous. The public was advised to keep its distance. If only I had heeded that sensible counsel.

Bashir was very excited. 'Did you hear what they called me?' he crowed. 'A criminal mastermind!' Despite our pleas he refused to eschew ostentation. On the contrary he pur-chased a Ferrari Testarossa, paid for with fat wads of hot money. He checked into Mayfair's poshest hotel and treated Fiona Bullfinch like a queen. I don't know when the police surveillance commenced, but it was certainly in place by the time of Pinkie's meeting with Bashir at the Hilton, at which large amounts of money exchanged hands. My inattentive flatmate returned after midnight, followed by a dozen uninvited guests. 'Well, well, well,' said one of the officers, rubbing his nose in time-honoured fashion, 'it seems that you people can't alter the habit of centuries, any more than a leopard can change its spots.' Bashir was arrested simultaneously. They took Fiona too. The hapless girl was humiliated when she finally understood that she was decked out in stolen finery, rather than the crown jewels of Iraq. That hurt her more than the charge of receiving stolen property.

Bashir was ready to own up at once, boasting to his captors that he had conceived, organized, and physically executed the most fantastic crime in living memory. He laughed when our haul was estimated at a mere twenty-five million. 'Nearer to forty,' he insisted. The authorities were inclined to believe him, reasoning that much of the loot was already contraband, and had therefore gone unrecorded. Only when it was pointed out that, under English law, the self-confessed Mr Big would not be required at the Old Bailey until sentence was passed, did Bashir shut up and change his plea from 'guilty as sin' to 'innocent as a virgin'. He was determined to make the most of his limited run at the law's equivalent of Westminster Abbey.

THE TRIAL WAS to be his coronation, the public acknowledgement of his achievement. Accordingly he turned up at court every morning dressed to kill, in Giorgio Armani suits and dark glasses. He flirted with the jury, lifting his Ray-Bans in order to wink at its prettier members. However, when I was called to the witness stand his antic manner was cast aside, to be replaced by a more sinister persona. As I raised my right hand and swore to tell the truth, he stared at me and slowly drew his index finger across his throat.

Not without justification, I confess. For I was about to describe the genesis of our conspiracy; naming names, and pinning the blame. I told how I had introduced Bashir to Pinkie, and how the pair of them had, once the ice was broken, drawn up a list of the most attractive propositions in London. The Kensington Safe Deposit Company was near the top and in Wasim, so Pinkie thought, they had an ideal open sesame. He explained about Wasim's financial problems – an operating loss of half a million, a personal overdraft in six figures – and suggested that, with a little persuasion, he would be a more than willing accomplice in the looting of his own company. So it proved. I joined because I was a smart-aleck.

However, I didn't feel so smart when the charges were listed and I realized that I was facing fifteen years in jail. My parents refused to see me, but swallowed their pride and went next door to beg their hoity-toity neighbours to send their son, a hot-shot lawyer, who grudgingly came and negotiated a much shorter sentence, provided I became an informer and gave evidence against my erstwhile colleagues. Noah no doubt would have agonized over the matter for days, wrestling with his conscience throughout the long confined nights; but to a simpler soul who knew there was no honour among thieves, the question was not moral but practical. Which was the more unbearable; incarceration or the threat of death? Well, we all live with the latter, and I had the advantage of knowing my enemy, unlike poor Charity who was surprised by her killer, that Lee Harvey

Oswald lurking in her genes. So I agreed to change sides. The move earned me five years instead of fifteen, and an investment in Fiona's womb. Lest I thought that I was getting off lightly the judge felt compelled to remind me that I would be looking over my shoulder for the rest of my life. Bashir, dressed in black, smiled like the angel of death. Now it's anybody's guess whether I'll die in prison or in some version of Ward No. 11.

After hearing his sentence Bashir thanked the judge. 'I have committed a serious crime,' he said, 'for which I will pay with the best years of my life. Even so I do not regret the choices I have made. To do so would be to gainsay the supreme moment of my career. Permit me to explain. When I cracked open those safe deposit boxes I felt godlike, as if my imagination had become manifest, as if I were creating what I found, each box revealing new ideas, a new touch of genius. Maybe I am a madman, but money was never my motive. I wanted to make a work of art, a crime that would live for ever in the minds of the masses. And I have done it; I have committed *la crème de la crime*. That is all I have to say. Now lock me away, I am satisfied.'

'Bashir's a lucky fellow,' I remark, 'I wish I could say the same.' I study Noah. 'You look like you could do with some yourself,' I say.

'Some what?' he asks.

'Satisfaction,' I reply.

Rosie laughs. 'Daddy's in the dumps,' she says. 'He kept very quiet about it, but I think he fell in love with my teacher, the beautiful Miss Tiptree. And now he's jealous, on account of a rumour going around that she's pregnant. It seems that a handsome stranger knocked on her door one day and never left. That's the story, at any rate. I hope it's true because it's so romantic.'

I could hug the girl, to have endured so much and not lost hope!

'Don't look so glum,' she says, 'we've brought you a present. Show him, Daddy.'

'Noah reveals a bag, marked Maxie's Meat Empire, from which he withdraws a scarlet slice of sirloin. 'For your eye,' he says, pointing to my latest shiner.

'Tell me, Noah,' I say, placing the raw meat over my swollen lid, 'what do you want out of life?'

'The same as Bashir,' he replies, 'to make a mark, to do one thing exceptionally well.'

I turn to Rosie and it occurs to me that, maybe, he has already achieved his ambition.

· PART II ·

My CV

ON MONDAYS, Wednesdays, and Fridays I work on my thesis, which modestly attempts to define the influence of Ovid upon the immortal Bard. On Tuesdays and Thursdays I sell cat food, viz., I write copy for a small advertising agency in Norwich.

It is Tuesday and there is a knock on the door. Two fellows in black coats are standing there. They give me the willies. Both look grave, like Mormons or sextons. In fact they are sexton blakes.

I have not yet been accused of anything, but already I am feeling guilty. I look at my hands. Oh God, I am still holding the pen! If they ask me what I am writing I shall have to tell them about my valiant efforts to shift a million tins of Catkins. This, in itself, is no crime. I only become a criminal when I accept money for my work. By failing to declare it I am, in effect, defrauding the government. If the authorities found out that I was moonlighting they would stop my grant immediately. I pray that the old Tupperware box, chock-a-block with my ill-gotten gains, is in its regular hiding place.

My visitors say nothing, obviously using psychological warfare to force a confession out of me. I try to look composed. Dear God, I pray, don't let me start to sweat.

When the plods finally come to the point I could hug the pair of them. 'We are conducting a murder inquiry,' they say, 'your mother said that we would find you here.' I bet she did! I can see her now, in her pink housecoat, pointing the way to 'my son, the murderer'. Put away your handcuffs, fellows, you've got the wrong man.

'Do you own a Citroën 2CV, sometimes called a Deux Chevaux?' they enquire.

'Yes,' I say, 'a yellow one.'

'The colour is immaterial,' they say, 'our witness spotted the car at night, when everything is either black or white.'

It turned out that gunmen had raided a garage at Cuckoo Bridge, near Spalding, Lincs., on Saturday night and shot the attendant through the heart. The only clue was a 2CV, seen parked nearby. What could the police do but interview every 2CV owner in the country, in the hope of trapping the guilty party?

Now I understood why my visitors (or colleagues just like them) had called on my mother. I had moved so many times in the years since leaving home that I continued to give it as my permanent address.

'Were you in Spalding last Saturday night?' they ask.

'No,' I say, 'I have never been to Lincolnshire in my life.'

After they have gone my wife suddenly appears and asks, 'Why did you lie?'

'I didn't,' I say.

'You said you've never been to Lincolnshire,' she says.

'That's the truth,' I protest.

'So where's Stamford?' she demands.

To make matters worse, we were there last Saturday, sleeping at the George.

My immediate reaction is to run after the cops and confess, but my wife persuades me otherwise. 'What difference,' she says, 'you're innocent.'

'So was Timothy Evans,' I reply.

Fortunately at that moment our son comes running into the house with a reprieve. 'Daddy,' he cries, 'I've just seen Shylock down the road.' Our son is only eight but (thanks to Charles Lamb) is already familiar with Hamlet, Othello, Macbeth, Romeo, and the aforementioned usurer. 'Come on, Dad,' he cries, 'before he goes.'

I have never been able to resist his charm. When I first set eyes upon his round face and his russet cheeks I determined to name him after our local apple, the St Edmund's Pippin, and so Pippin it was. He was such a beautiful baby I began to fear for his safety. Sure enough, when he was eighteen months, a common cold turned nasty. 'No need to drive through red traffic lights,' said our general practitioner, 'but don't dawdle either.' Blood tests revealed an abnormally low sodium count. A pathologist was urgently summoned from his home to examine the results of a lumbar puncture. No, it wasn't meningitis. Next day Pippin was swaddled in bandages and made to sweat in a broiling room. It wasn't cystic fibrosis either. The final diagnosis came as something of a relief; asthma. Since then it has been hard to refuse him anything. I let him take me by the hand and lead me down Eastgate Street, to where the theatrical gentleman is gently swaying in the road. Who needs cat food anyway?

'There he is!' cries Pippin, pointing to a decidedly incongruous figure positioned outside the Fox. The Jews hereabouts are mostly like Moyses Hall, the oldest house in the city. It was built by the Normans, some say for a Jew. They claim that a niche in an eastern wall had once accommodated an ark. Who knows? Either way the house has become so assimilated over the centuries that it is no longer possible to be certain of its origins. At present it is a museum and contains such treasures as a copy of *Murder in the Red Barn* bound in the flayed hide of the heartless assassin. Pippin is a frequent visitor.

His Jew is facing the flinty walls of the Abbey, beyond which are the ruins of the noble edifice where Henry VI once held his parliament (vide *Henry VI, Part 2*, act III).

'Well?' he says, smiling triumphantly.

'That's not Shylock,' I laugh, 'it's a common or garden Hassid.'

'A what?' Pippin asks.

'A Jew who thinks he's still in Poland,' I reply.

'Are they all as bad as Shylock?' asks my boy. (I'm afraid that Shakespeare's ambiguity is lost on an eight-year-old.)

'Of course not!' I say.

'Daddy,' says Pippin, 'what's that funny scarf around his neck?'

'It's a *tallit*,' I say.

'What's that?' he asks.

'A prayer shawl,' I reply.

'Why is the man rocking backwards and forwards?' Pippin asks.

'He's praying,' I reply.

'What for?' asks Pippin. 'And why is he praying in the middle of the street?'

'I don't know,' I say, 'perhaps he's saying *kaddish*.'

'What's *kaddish*?' asks Pippin. 'Is it a vegetable? Is there a horse-*kaddish*?'

'Don't be silly,' I say, 'it's a prayer for the dead.'

'Has someone died?' asks Pippin.

'Not recently,' I reply. 'Hundreds of years ago there was a Jewish community in Bury St Edmunds. The Abbot owed them a lot of money, which he didn't want to repay. So he told a pack of wicked lies about them. Unfortunately the people swallowed the lot.'

'What happened?' asks my boy.

'Nothing very nice,' I reply. 'Most of the Jews were murdered, the remainder fled for their lives.'

'Was the Abbot ever punished?' asks my innocent boy.

'On the contrary,' I say, 'he is regarded as the saviour of the Abbey to this day.'

'Daddy,' asks Pippin, 'how come you know so much about Jews?'

'I used to live among them,' I reply.

My wife is still standing in the doorway of our half-timbered cottage (which once featured on the cover of a calendar published by the Eastern Daily Press). She beckons us and we stroll home, hugging the bosky bank of the River Linnet, our progress mirrored by a bald coot and its chick.

Pippin is a curious child, as you have seen, which is why

we elected to take him on a brief tour of his heritage, including Shakespeare's birthplace and (by way of balance) Ironbridge, the cradle of the Industrial Revolution.

We drove north-west across the black fenlands in our yellow 2CV, until we spied Ely Cathedral, calling to us like a lighthouse. From there we took a minor road to Peterborough, visited the tomb of Catherine of Aragon, and continued along the Great North Road to Stamford. Somehow I missed the county markers. Had anyone asked me I would have guessed that I was in Huntingdonshire or, at a pinch, Rutland. What's the difference?

We took a room at the George, which still has the leathery glamour of an old coaching inn. Wandering through the bar we spotted one Uriah Heep lookalike, the double of Wackford Squeers, and two dead ringers for Mr Pickwick. We had dinner (guinea fowl, venison, and roast suckling pig), liqueurs, and then retired for the night.

As a matter of fact the road always makes me restless. Being unable to sleep I reached under the sheet for my wife. 'Stop it,' she whispered, 'how can we make love in front of Pippin? He might wake up, if he isn't awake already.'

'So what?' I hissed. 'He's got to learn the facts of life sooner or later.'

'You're disgusting,' she replied.

Actually I was furious. I quit the bed, dressed, and wandered the streets of Stamford in a frenzy of frustration. I felt out of time and out of place, like a werewolf or some other horrible anachronism. The local limestone glowed eerily in the moonlight, as I marched from All Saints' Place to Barn Hill, without meeting a living soul. Clocks in church spires struck midnight, one, two ... When I eventually returned my wife and Pippin were both fast asleep.

Leaving Stamford we motored west across the Midlands, ignoring signs to Coalville, Coleshill, Sutton Coldfield, and passing countless empty factories with dilapidated walls and broken windows. Middle England was clearly depressed. Pippin sat on the back seat, in happy ignorance, listening to Roald Dahl on his Walkman.

A joker or anarchist was active in the vicinity of Brownhills; thereabouts every 'To Let' had its infinitive split by an extraneous vowel, the ubiquitous 'i'.

Telford was a different world; a new town whose history was being underwritten by Japanese and American corporations. It looked like the handiwork of invaders, not immigrants; the modern equivalent of a Norman castle. The indigenous infrastructure – long since redundant – was preserved as a World Heritage Site at nearby Ironbridge. The eponymous bridge arched gracefully above the River Severn, like a gateway to some rural idyll, rather than the entrance to some long dormant hell-hole, over which the Bedlam Furnaces once glowered like pocket-sized Popocatepetls.

We found a room at the Tontine Hotel, built in 1784 at the behest of the Iron Bridge's hard-boiled shareholders. A tontine, by the way, is an annuity shared by subscribers to a loan, individual shares increasing as subscribers die, leaving the pot to the last survivor. If I were a sexton blake I'd be keeping an eye on such legalized invitations to murder, rather than harassing innocent travellers who happen to drive foreign cars.

That night I was afflicted yet again with insomnia, and

once more turned to my wife for comfort. Again she slapped my hand. 'What are you, an animal?' she snapped. 'Can't you control your urges for a couple of nights?'

The next day we both took Pippin to Blists Hill, 'a re-created working community', which boasted its own railway siding, red clay mine, ironworks, and candle factory. I walked through it all in a daze.

After lunch we crossed the river to Jackfield, to visit the Tile Museum. It was there that an unsettling incident occurred.

Once upon a time the tiles were designed in an ecclesiast-ical-style structure with cruciform windows and wooden floors. Alongside the galleries (now full of objets d'art) were offices where clerks in starched collars prepared invoices and balanced the books, where straight-laced secretaries typed letters on new-fangled machines, and where the directors entertained their valued clients.

The portraits on the walls were of patriarchal types with mutton-chop sideboards. They consolidated Victoria's empire by laying tiles that were attractive, economical, and, above all, hygienic. Just as the politicians relied on Tommy Atkins to do their dirty work, so these Gradgrinds sat in padded chairs while labourers sweated on their behalf in the adjacent factory.

A guide led us around the abandoned site. If I had known her better (or had had more confidence in my charm) I would have tucked in the label that protruded above the collar of her blouse. An unseasonable wind loosened a few strands of her grey hair. It whistled down the open corridor between the two terraces of brick-built workshops.

'These old buildings may look run down,' she said, 'but in their heyday they housed a very efficient process. Do you see those blue doors at the far end of the yard?' We all looked. 'Well, they opened at the beginning of every working day to admit a new consignment of clay. The clay itself was taken from the hills. That's how it went, day after day. In one end as clay, out the other as finished tiles. Once the clay was inside the yard the selection process began. It was pounded into dust, and then graded according to its grain. It was all stored in these buildings to our right.' We began walking between the rows.

'The buildings to our left accommodated the kilns,' continued our guide. 'Unfortunately they are derelict now, and too dangerous to enter. In fact the whole of the gorge is slipping into the river at a rate of five centimetres every year. Half of Jackfield has already gone, not to mention its road and railway line. This whole site will disappear too, in the fullness of time. Don't worry, it won't happen today, but as a precaution I must ask you to look through the windows and imagine the kilns roaring away like giant beehives.'

We all stared at the circular foundations of the great ovens, broken at regular intervals to allow for the doors. Two fans (built into the walls) continued to rotate, even though the heat was no more than a memory.

Our guide explained that much of the old machinery, and some of the intact buildings, had been leased to a team of modern tile makers, on the understanding that they allowed visitors to observe them at work.

One of their number, a young man, with long hair and

the hint of a moustache, demonstrated how the powdered clay, as fine as bonemeal, was poured into a mould and compressed by a machine that delivered a punch weighing fifteen tons. It emerged as a proto-tile, ready for baking.

'Of course, I am proceeding very cautiously,' remarked the young man, passing his handiwork around, 'in the good old days this press would have been pounding away nonstop. The men had to be quick, getting the clay in and their hands out before the piston dropped, otherwise it was bye-bye fingers.' He wiggled his, to prove that they were all still there.

'What were conditions like for the workers?' asked my wife (if only she showed a similar concern for my welfare).

'Terrible,' he replied. 'The lucky ones crushed their fingers and got out early. The remainder contracted emphysema or some other lung disease. Needless to say, masks were never worn. Despite the conditions, they were capable of turning out six million tiles per annum. So many, in fact, that the ovens couldn't cope.'

We returned to the wind and the derelict buildings, whereupon Pippin suddenly began to wheeze, as though the ancient poison had infiltrated his lungs. 'Daddy!' he gasped. 'I can't breathe!' I felt helpless, oppressed by history, not even able to provide my son with clean air. 'Take this,' said my wife calmly, handing him his Ventolin.

'Now you know how the poor workmen must have felt,' said our sympathetic guide. Wishing to leave him with happier memories she pointed to an external staircase built of wood. 'Do you see that?' she asked. 'It was used by Sir David Lean in his film of *Oliver Twist* to represent the entrance to Fagin's den. You've heard of Fagin, haven't you, my dear?' Poor Pippin nodded. I looked and for a second I swear I saw the image of the Hasid on the top step. He had a noose around his neck.

On Monday the weather broke. We queued to enter Anne Hathaway's Cottage in the pouring rain and decided to call it a day. The sexton blakes came on Tuesday.

On Wednesday they return the call. 'Refresh our memory,' they say. 'What reason did you give for going to Spalding?'

'I didn't,' I say, 'I've never been there.'

'But you also stated that you had never visited Lincoln-shire,' they say, 'when the hotel register at the George tells a different story.'

'That was a mistake,' I reply, 'I didn't know that Stamford was in Lincolnshire.'

'English geography not your strong point, eh, Mr Cowan?' they say mockingly.

They are gone, but they will be back, of that I am sure. And next time they'll have a search warrant. Then what? They'll find the loot, which I won't be able to explain away. And they'll discover that my alibi isn't watertight, that I went walkabout for more than two hours in the depths of Saturday night . . . precisely when the crime was committed.

I cannot sleep, I lie in bed waiting for the knock on the door.

It comes, as anticipated, early on Friday morning. 'You go,' says my wife, 'it must be the postman.' There is a second bang, much louder than the first.

'Daddy,' cries Pippin, 'there's someone at the door.'

'I'll go,' says my wife, putting on her dressing gown.

'No,' I cry, knocking her to the ground. I run to Pippin's room and lift him from the bed. 'There is no time,' I cry, 'the antisemites are without. We must hide!'

The Iceman Cometh

'ZUNI! *Zoo-knee!*' There is a note of panic in that summons which causes me to cast aside the newspaper (with its anodyne digest of local scandals) and rush towards the bathroom. Maya, my wife, is within, sitting white faced in the bath. She has the punctured gravitas of an ice queen whose throne has unaccountably melted. 'Has something happened?' I ask, checking the water. No worries there; it is immaculate, kosher, not a blood-spot in sight. So why the panic? 'Listen,' Maya whispers, pointing to the radio, which is perched on the edge of the tub like an extraterrestrial parakeet. It mimics our language to perfection, but its *Weltanschauung* is back-to-front, as though it were observing the world in a mirror. Thus it calmly informs us that pacific Ashkenazia has invaded bellicose Ishmalyia. The other-worldly voice proceeds to explain why this war is different from all other wars. In all other wars soldiers advance with the intention of annihilating the enemy, but in this war *au contraire* our boys are only fighting to save the body politic. The army of Ashkenazia is like a surgeon, committed to the excision of a life-threatening tumour. The operation –

operation being the operative word – is code-named Peace Now.

'There wasn't a word in today's paper,' I complain, 'not even a hint.' I look at my own hands. It seems that I will be compelled to abandon the tools of my trade – I am a sculptor – in order to take up arms yet again, if only a scalpel.

'Hold me, Zuni,' cries my wife, 'I am frightened.' She is also wet. So what? It is June; it is a hot day.

My wife is frightened of cataclysms, both natural and man-made; she fears the flood, the tempest, and the quake, she fears the heat of the sun, the dread lightning-flash, and bloody war. As for the quotidian, that she takes in her stride, being blessed with unquestioning faith in her body and its equilibrium. I am the opposite (though I also worship her body); I cringe from the enemy within, the unseen worm in the bud. My credo is borrowed from Paul Klee, 'To stand despite all possibilities to fall.' Maya comforts me when unaccountable ailments assail my frame; gives me motherly comfort when my nose haemorrhages, my heart skips a beat, or a critic stabs me in the back. Today, however, it is my turn to be the Rock of Gibraltar. Like some ancient patriarch with a hotline to Jehovah I hug my beautiful, frightened, pregnant wife, murmuring sweet assurances, while the radio continues to parrot its perverse song.

I FIRST MET MAYA nine years ago, a few months after the last battle with the Ishmaelites. One of the happier consequences of that near catastrophe.

It happened that I had been invited, by the Minister of Culture no less, to design a memorial for those who had fallen in the late war. Excuse me, I do not wish to draw attention to my achievements, but it is a fact that my work – even then – was held in high esteem. 'The brief is simplicity itself,' the Minister explained. 'We want to celebrate a miracle – how else can you describe the way our boys turned certain defeat into victory? – but to celebrate with tears not champagne. We want to acknowledge the triumph, but also its cost; the price our people paid in precious blood.' He paused. 'What we require is a kind of font. I'm not talking literally, of course – I mean a place where our people can renew the collective memory and refresh our nation's will. We want everyone who sees the memorial to experience, if only vicariously, the trauma of those terrible weeks – in short, to become Ashkenazim on the spot.'

'Tell me,' scoffed Dr Hopi, when I reported the conversation to him, 'exactly how one *renews* a memory. In the same way as one retouches a photograph, or rewrites history? I concede that amnesia is a curse, but I am equally convinced that the sanctification of memory is a dangerous fetish. Politicians, like your fat friend, are trying to turn it into a sort of national DNA.' Dr Hopi, a bald psychiatrist with radical views, was the voice of my conscience, my very own Jiminy Cricket.

Inca, another crony, took a more worldly view. 'Go for it,' he said, picking crumbs from his beard. Inca was a journalist, a political columnist. Dr Hopi snorted with derision. No surprise; Hopi and Inca never agreed about anything. The three of us were old schoolfriends, and we edited an occasional magazine called *The Optimist*, not because any of us were, but because we liked a joke some

Bulgarian immigrants had brought with them from the mother country. It went something like this. Do you know the difference between a Bulgarian optimist and a Bulgarian pessimist? No? Well, the pessimist says, 'Things are so bad they cannot get any worse.' To which the optimist replies, 'Oh yes they can.'

I followed Inca's advice and accepted the commission. My problem thereafter was to find a way of distilling our national experience into a single image. Since our history is essentially a dialogue between martyrdom and renaissance I thought immediately of the phoenix, the bird that rises triumphantly from its own funeral pyre. At the same time I did not want to produce a simple allegory. And so I determined to steer a way between the Scylla and Charybdis of abstraction and kitsch. I wanted to make a forceful statement that would provoke an immediate emotional response. Pity, yes. But more than pity . . . something positive . . . exhortation, yes. Exhortation and . . . why not? . . . exultation.

I photographed the site, an empty square in the heart of Ashkenaz's diplomatic quarter. Then I spread the prints on the worktop in my studio and began gumming pictures clipped from magazines over the vacant lot. I made sketches of the superimpositions that caught my fancy, producing countless variations upon each theme. One, in particular, began to appear more and more frequently.

Just before the war – in late September, to be precise – marine archaeologists had plucked a Greek bronze from the seabed. It was the life-size statue of an ephebe, an Athenian youth, wearing nothing but a *chlamys*. Restored (like its adopted nation) it had been placed on display at the termination of hostilities, and was now the main attraction at the Maritime Museum in Moho, ninety miles away on the Mediterranean coast. Hence the numerous articles. I devoured the pictures. I even drove to Moho to view the thing in the flesh. There was no doubt, it was a masterpiece; completely intact, save for absent pedal extremities. Unable to stand upon his own feet the crippled boy had been mounted on metal prosthetics. It was this detail which caught my attention, for the statue was clearly not correctly counterpoised. It was leaning too far forwards. In other words, it should have fallen over. Returning to my sketch-books I began to toy with the idea of a naked female, similarly defiant of gravity.

At the same time I plundered my shelves, which were stocked with home-made replicas of indigenous common-places and curiosities: amphorae, anchors, angels, boats, bones, centaurs, dolphins, figs, grapes, guitars, kitchen knives, leaves, lemons, limbs, Minotaurs, nereids, oranges, Pans, pears, plants, pomegranates, shells, tears, torsos, and Zeus – my own clay alphabet. I assembled little groups, the most interesting of which I juxtaposed with the ideas already in the sketchbooks. At last I came up with a proposal.

A young woman stands, like the ephebe, with the aid of calipers. She too is naked. At her feet (or rather around the spot where her tootsies should be) are ruptured pomegran-ates. The ground is dark, stained red by the spilled grena-dine. However, six of the pips have germinated, are bursting with life renewed. They are watered by the girl's salty tears. I made a scaled-down maquette and presented it to the

Minister. He wept. Why not? His only son had been horribly disfigured in one of the terrible tank battles. 'Just as the best grapes grow at the mouth of the volcano,' he said, wiping his eyes, 'so does great art flourish in an age of fire and brimstone.'

Bohemian Ashkenaz was full of women who would remove their clothes for a fee, but I needed someone new, an innocent who could move without self-consciousness; an Eve before the Fall, spontaneity personified. In the meantime I purchased a crate of rosy pomegranates from the famous orchards of Alfa, a village in a fertile valley a morning's drive from Ashkenaz. There was, as ever, a label on the box featuring Princess Yum Yum; a dark-skinned girl with plaited chestnut hair, upon which rested a wreath of avocado leaves. Threaded kernels hung around her neck, and an overflowing cornucopia rested on her lap. But where was my own Princess Yum Yum, the muse who would bless my work as Yum Yum blessed the fruit of Alfa?

Unable to commence I took to wandering around the city, making a melancholy progress from memorial to memorial. Some stood abandoned, as if their original purpose had been forgotten by all, nothing now but inert disjunctures in the cityscape; while others attracted perpetual mourners, who left stones or candles or bunches of flowers. On a mild night in December I happened to pause beside a monument that honoured the three captains tortured to death by the Ishmaelites in '48. At its centre was a seated man with an unsheathed sword across his lap, wearing nothing but a pained expression on his face. Beside him was the dedication, inscribed in letters of gold on a large wall. I was alone, save for a young woman who seemed to be addressing the naked icon.

I assumed she was reciting a prayer, a *kaddish* for the departed, but her expression seemed incongruous. Mourners rarely smile. Curious, I listened. 'Serves you right,' she was whispering confidentially to the dead hero, 'if you choose to sit on a stone bench without any trousers you deserve to get a dose of haemorrhoids.' It was none of my business, but I couldn't hold my tongue.

'It's all very well to be clever,' I snapped, 'but you must remember that the sculptor was doing a difficult job. In its day this piece, which you find so amusing, was probably a sensation. A courageous break from the style of his elders and betters.'

'Why are you so upset?' she asked. 'Are you related to any of the dead?'

'No,' I said, 'I'm a sculptor.'

'Not *the* sculptor?' she said.

'Hardly,' I replied, 'he's long gone. But I would, nevertheless, like to hear why you think his work is such a hoot.'

'Perhaps I was wrong to mock,' she conceded, 'but I find it hard to take the thing seriously. To me it's less a memorial, more a fanciful reflection of Ashkenazia's self-image. The man is naked and vulnerable, but muscular too. Yes, I notice such things. He sits like Rodin's thinker – post-thought. His expression says that the time for meditation is over. The unsheathed sword, held horizontally, will shortly become tumescent. He is, in effect, the ideal Ashkenazi male; the virile intellectual about to confront our eternal enemy.'

The girl was no fool. She wasn't ugly either. 'I didn't

mean to snap,' I replied, 'I just overheard what you were saying and suddenly felt a bit protective. I know it wasn't meant personally, but for a moment I felt that the whole of our profession was under fire. A bit of an overreaction, I admit. Can I make amends and buy you a coffee?'

I led her to the Café des Artistes. Where else? She took off her coat, ordered an espresso, and — with a little prompting — told me her story. Like the pomegranates she hailed from the village of Alfa. Indeed her parents were founder members of the settlement. Those hardy pioneers had been attracted by the sweet water, which glittered like quicksilver, the luxuriant rushes, and the wild palms with their golden dates. They cultivated the land and planted rows of peaches, almonds, pistachios, pomegranates, and alligator pears which, in the fullness of time, bore fruit. They also raised children, surely none more beautiful than my companion. 'Alfa was like Paradise,' she said, 'but it could not contain me. I had eaten of every tree in the village, and was ready to suck strange juices, ones that were only available in the distant city on a hill.' She sipped her coffee. 'So I made the ascent,' she said, licking the bitter tidemark from her lips. But life at the top was not easy. She had been in Ashkenaz for three months, she confessed, and still had not found her feet. Her figure was Greek, her complexion unblemished, her rural innocence untarnished by the cynicism of metropolitan life. I asked if she wanted a job. She accepted. That's how I met Maya.

She turned out to be a wonderful model, a natural. Not only could she move with the perpetual grace of a ballerina, she also possessed a protean imagination. 'There has been a metamorphosis,' I would say, 'you are now an animal, a fish, a plant – whatever you fancy.' Needless to say the alteration was invisible to the naked eye. No matter! I saw with my hand, which moved autonomously across the paper. (Only when I had completed the sketch could I recognize the nature of her temporary incarnation. 'You have changed into a cheetah!' I would cry. Or a tree. Or whatever . . .) When I placed a lump of damp clay upon the rotating stand Maya likewise began to pirouette, until there were no definable boundaries between her corpus and the world. Round and round she went, sheathed in gold by a shower of light, while I tried to reproduce her splendour in a fistful of mud.

The following summer the bronze was cast and the completed statue unveiled. The Minister of Culture made a speech, bereaved parents wailed. Even Dr Hopi was impressed.

'Congratulations,' he cried, pumping my hand, 'it is a triumph. You know my opinion concerning ersatz memorials, but this is the real thing. Why? Because it does not attempt to prompt precisely the same memory in everyone. You have recognized, if only unconsciously, that a unified form of commemoration is not the same as the unification of memory. I salute you.' Before I had time to respond Inca grabbed my arm. 'She's a peach!' he exclaimed. 'Not a dead surface in sight. She's alive from her zygoma to her knees. What's more she's got tits to die for. Tell me, maestro, is she real or did you dream her up?'

'She is real,' I replied, 'and I propose to marry her.'

WE DROVE TO MOHO for our honeymoon. In fact I hired a four-cylinder Zorro with a soft-top for the occasion.

If you have ever visited our country you'll be familiar with
Ashkenaz and be aware that it suddenly ceases. It has no
suburbs, nor outskirts. One minute you are in a congested
city street, the next there is nothing but the sirocco gusting
through the dry valleys with their toy-town villages and the
jasmin-scented air. The scorching wind knotted our hair as
we sailed joyously along the open road. Later, when we entered
the pine forests, cooler breezes carried a turpentiny tang, as
astringent as aftershave. We sped through the fertile central
valley like exiled royalty, turning the turbanned heads of
Ishmaelite orange-pickers. Then we ascended again and,
rounding the final hairpin, at last saw the floating city of
Moho, suspended on waves of heat. It looked like a mirage.

Our hotel was a white villa. Red-hot braziers seemed to
be hanging from every window, so fiery were the geraniums
on display. The receptionist handed us a key. We entered
our room. It had a bay view. The light was blinding. The sun
fell upon the sea like glass, shattering on impact. We fell
upon the bed. Every morning we took the short cut to the
beach, winding our way down an overgrown path lined with
pompons of powdery yellow mimosa. Reaching the esplan-
ade we laid out our towels upon the broiling sand, and oiled
our bodies. Sometimes we swam, or picked our way between
the fractured columns and shattered marble floors which still
littered the shoreline. Ancient Moho had once been a major
port. It was constructed by our ancestors upon the ruins of
an even older Moho, destroyed by an earthquake in the year
dot. The second Moho was flattened in its turn, but the
harbour remained, its immortal jetties still protecting the
beach from the depredations of the remorseless surf.

No less persistent were the convalescent officers, with their swashbuckling eyepatches and glamorous limps. Drawn by Maya's beauty they arrived bearing floral tributes, and stayed to test her fidelity with their heroic narratives. After a few days I actually began to regret that I had not been wounded in action, or at least performed some act of derring-do. 'You must not be jealous,' Maya whispered one airless night, whilst we were making love, 'they are just boys. You – you are my man.' Nevertheless I couldn't help but envision her drifting away across the tiles in the scarred arms of a uniformed suitor. It wasn't that I doubted her word, it was just that she seemed so *unearthed*, as though she needed to be tethered to the ground like a Zeppelin. But I did not marry her to be her anchor, let alone her ball and chain; I married her because of that very quality, that hint of helium in the bloodstream. Consequently I could do nothing but trust her. Easier said than done!

One afternoon in a green-eyed huff I separated myself from Maya's admirers and, standing on the shoreline, studied the eternal motion of the sea. Ask people to name the sea's opposite and they will invariably answer *terra firma*. Wrong! How wrong they are! Dry land is no more stable than the oceans. It too is in constant motion. It spins through space, while tectonic plates shift within. The aborigines of Mesoamerica, making a virtue out of radical instability, based their world-view upon the ever-present possibility of destruction. To them history was no continuum, rather a series of advances and reverses, a succession of catastrophes and renewals; in short, a sort of cosmic snakes and ladders. I am no Indian, but it makes sense to me.

Nor is anything upon the earth ever static. Fruit ripens, light alters, what is here today will be gone tomorrow. As for our bodies ... they are like the *I Ching*. Even when we die the changes do not cease. 'Please,' said an oriental tourist, pointing his camera at me. I obligingly took a snap of the whole family, a souvenir of Moho. Sculpture is not like photography; it does not seek to arrest movement or stop time. Hardly! Sculpture exists to celebrate transience. That is why the great works of Michelangelo and Rodin throb with kinetic energy. Maya was their living sister, loaned to me by some beneficent deity for an unknown period. In exchange I would have to accept the possibility of a whimsical divorce, even on our honeymoon. Suddenly seized with the desire to create a memento amore I sought a stretch of beach that had not already been annexed by a miniature Imhotep, and there began to mould a life-size replica of my wife out of the dampened sand.

My concentration was finally broken by a squeal from the original. 'Zuni, come and join us! We're all going to have ice creams!' She sounded as excited as a little girl. I arose, brushed the sand off my legs, and arrived to find four eager conscripts vying for the honour of paying for her strawberry cornet. The ice-cream seller, who orbited the beach as predictably as Halley's Comet, carried a small iceberg on a tray, around which were clustered multicoloured tubs and a rainbow of lollipops. It kept his merchandise frozen, but it also obscured his view, and was the probable cause of his fall, which occurred when he tripped over the fragile reproduction of my beloved, and thereby reduced her to a billion golden molecules.

My apprehensions were unfounded. Maya has remained with me for nine years, faithful, so I believe, both as model and wife. At least there is no evidence of moonlighting, or of clandestine engagements in the nude. And now, as proof of our successful synthesis, she is manufacturing a child, juggling genes in her womb. A slight swelling is already visible as she steps out of the bath. I hand her a towel. At the same time there is a rap at the front door. It is the captain of my unit. As I feared my services are required in Ishmalyia. I am ordered to leave immediately. Maya weeps. 'Come back,' she says, 'I don't want to be the widow of a dead hero.'

I kiss her. 'Look after our baby,' I say.

I CROSS THE BORDER that very afternoon. There are the same fields on the other side, the same crops, the same mountains, the same seascapes, the same dramatic sky. Only the roads are bumpier. War is not a separate state; it is to the quotidian as the drivers of Ishmalyia are to our own law-abiding motorists. War is life with your foot pressed down on the accelerator, life without rules, life with the possibility of death at every corner. What may take a century in normal circumstances can be accomplished in a few belligerent moments. Entire generations can vanish, cities fall. 'If we don't get killed,' I say, 'we may even benefit from this fiasco. Life will seem that much sweeter.'

'For you, perhaps,' snaps Inca, staring grimly out of the window of the bus that is transporting us to the battlefields, 'but I doubt if the poor sods who once lived in those pock-marked hovels will thank us for the learning experience.'

'For once I agree with our friend,' says Dr Hopi, who is

sitting behind. 'Has our Minister of Defence, the veteran of numerous campaigns, benefited from his adventures? Is he a wiser man? Can pigs fly? If he were my patient I'd have him certified on the spot. Only a madman would have attacked Ishmalyia.'

We make camp on a hill overlooking orchards and the sea. My colleagues suck oranges and exchange gossip with the troops we're replacing. 'If you were wondering where to buy cheap watches, perfume and cigarettes, I know just the place,' says Inca, who homes in on such titbits as surely as swine scent truffles. We are served meat loaf for dinner, sardines on toast for breakfast. The distance from morning to evening equals the distance from here to the horizon. I begin to think that I am wrong about universal instability, that there is at least one place in the world where everything is fixed (including the clock) and that I am in the middle of it. I take an eternity to telephone Maya, and almost as long to rearrange my belongings in our tent. Inca and Hopi are no quicker. They are too bored even to argue.

Occasionally we pile into a Zelda and patrol the coastal road, on the lookout for the enemy. What enemy? The kids wave, and the local farmers inch up the hill in their tractors, eager to sell us vegetables and fruit. In fact the only dangers are accidental; we could roll over, if the incline is steeper than expected, or we could hit a landmine (which would certainly be catastrophic, since we're sitting on a ton of high explosives). Otherwise we are safe. By way of compensation there are countless rumours. 'Don't listen to them,' counsels Inca, 'unless you want to go mad.' To demonstrate their unreliability he makes an outrageous joke. It quickly becomes a rumour. Two hours later it's repeated to us as fact. Nevertheless, one story persists; that we've be chosen to lead the assault on Ishmalyia City. It sounds convincing, especially when we are sent to a nearby village and ordered to practise house to house fighting. We are well rehearsed; the journalist throws a grenade through the door, the sculptor bursts in shooting, the psychiatrist gallops up the stairs. The locals shake their heads. It is said that another unit has hired two girls from this place to service their needs for the duration. I do not blame them; the girls are certainly pretty, with their black hair, sweet faces, and tight jeans. Speculation continues. 'How many of us are likely to die if we go in?' wonders Dr Hopi. 'One in three is the estimate,' replies Inca.

Between our camp and the village is a river. It comes off the mountain and is so clean you could bottle it. On quiet days we are permitted to bathe there. We embrace the water as eagerly as Hedy Lamarr, stark naked save for our M16s (which can fire even after immersion). Inca is squat, muscular, and hairy. 'Have you ever noticed,' I remark to Dr Hopi, 'that our esteemed comrade bears a remarkable resemblance to a centaur?' As if to prove otherwise Inca performs some handstands midstream, much to the admiration of several indigenous lads. They strip down to their underpants, push aside the bulrushes and paddle towards us. 'What do they want?' I say. It turns out they want to know just one thing; whether sex is permissible between males in Ashkenazia. 'Certainly,' I reply, 'though we three are happily married, thank you very much. Indeed my wife is expecting a baby.'

As I speak I observe, out of the corner of my eye, some movement between the trees that are scattered around the nearby meadows like sunshades at a private swimming pool. Holding my gun under the water I carefully release the safety catch. My finger feels for the trigger. I take deep breaths, and hope that I am not going to panic; that I will shoot the enemy, rather than my friends. Then I see that the bushwhacker, the approaching assassin, is actually one of our boys. He looks terrified, poor thing. 'Zuni!' he is calling. 'Zuni! Who is Zuni?'

I wave, then wade to the water's edge. 'What's up?' I say. 'Are we invading Ishmalyia City after all?'

'No,' he says, 'it's your wife.' He looks at his feet.

'Well?' I say.

'She's had a miscarriage,' he replies.

At first I experience this absurd relief that it is not the expected summons to some horrible and bloody engagement. Of course I am fully aware that this is an inappropriate response, and do my best to look like a man who has just been apprised of a personal tragedy. 'Do not mind us,' says Dr Hopi, who has torn himself away from the curious Ishmaelites, 'cry if that is what you feel like doing. You must not suppress your emotions. It is important that you grieve.' But for what? An unborn child I never saw, and hardly had time to imagine. No, I cannot weep; nor do I really know the grief that Hopi has prescribed. *Disappointment* is *le mot juste*; I have been hollowed out, as though robbed of a major commission, leaving me with nothing but a still-born idea. As far as I am concerned *miscarriage* means missing the bus to some unknown destination. Instead I catch the next one home to Ashkenaz.

IT IS DIFFERENT for Maya, and for me, when I find her prostrate and bloodless in a hospital bed. 'I saw him, our little boy,' she says weeping, 'he was perfect, a perfect little corpse.' What irony is here! I have been to war and not encountered a single dead body, whereas Maya − safe and sound at home − has had to face the ultimate horror. Moreover, thanks to television, she has been forced to witness the consequences of my actions (yes, I share the guilt, even though I knew nothing). She tells how the bombardment of Ishmalyia City made her sick to the stomach. 'For years my parents assured me that our innate helplessness prevented us from doing evil,' she says. 'The world, they explained, was run by carnivores, and we were mice, the lowest of the low. If we were lucky we nibbled cheese, certainly not chunks of our neighbour's territory. But now the United Nations calls us the Hammer of the Ishmaelites and I cannot say that they are wrong. My parents lied to me, Zuni. We are monsters!'

Nurse Lovic, a comely midwife, beckons me to her side. 'Heaven forbid that I add to the woes of your lovely wife by making her think that she is responsible for this affliction,' she whispers, 'but if you want my opinion your son was as much a war victim as any dead soldier. Let me tell you something else,' she adds in an even more confidential tone, 'your wife is by no means alone in her predicament. In fact these days there are more miscarriages than live births − especially of boys. It's as though women have become too scared to bring them into the world, not wishing to breed another – how shall I put it? – another fraternity of murderers.'

'I'm afraid that our Nurse Lovic is something of a Manichean,' says Dr Zecs the obstetrician, 'in that she blames our gender for everything.' He wraps a patrician arm around my shoulder. 'However, she is right in one respect,' he continues. 'There does seem to be a new syndrome at large which is unaccountably causing the *male* foetus to spontaneously abort in the fourth month of pregnancy.' He pauses, gives my plebeian bicep a squeeze, and attempts to sweeten the pill. 'Rest assured, some of the best minds in Ashkenazia are trying to find out why – our own Professor Zunz foremost among them. I do not want to raise false hopes, but it seems that he is very close to an explanation. It goes something like this . . . Ashkenazi males have always carried one copy of an abnormal gene which, if not de-activated, automatically precipitates self-destruction. Fortu-nately, we remained in happy ignorance of this fact for nearly two millennia, because the dominant healthy gene, carried by the mother, invariably overrode its malign prompting. Alas, for some reason this is no longer the case. The failsafe has failed.' He laughs. 'Don't look so miserable,' he adds, 'you have my word that the fault is only temporary.'

Nurse Lovic snorts. 'I've already told him that withdrawal is the only solution,' she grumbles. 'Just give us peace and I'll guarantee a new generation of malefactors.'

'You say that Professor Zunz has isolated the cause,' I look at Nurse Lovic, 'the *remote origins* at any rate. But how about a cure? Has he discovered that?'

'Not yet,' concedes Dr Zecs.

'So what happens if we want another child?' I ask.

'You'll have to hope that it's a girl,' he replies.

Though depressed Maya is deemed to have recovered and is discharged. I take her home. The house is the same, but she is a changed woman. I mean this literally. We are living through an age of miraculous transformations, when countries replicate like amoeba, and political structures disappear overnight, so why shouldn't a woman suddenly develop a new personality? Mercurial Maya has turned into a couch potato. Day after day she wears the same T-shirt, with a dove across her breasts. Nothing else. Her legs are unshaven, her hair unkempt. Her body odour makes my eyes water. From morning to night she watches television, keening like a pro while the bad news is broadcast (as it is every hour on the hour). When she isn't watching television she is listening to the radio, ferrying it from the kitchen via the bedroom to the bathroom. Meanwhile I attempt to work in my studio.

An impossibility! My imagination has been invaded, the space that should be filled with a gallery of future works is now colonized by images of dead babies and the atrocities of war. I am tempted to turn them into a metaphor of some description, if only to clear my mind, but the dead refuse to grant the necessary permission. 'We have been robbed of our lives,' they say, 'please do not steal our individuality as well.' I make sketches instead, but they all look like photographs and are torn up.

Tension fills the house like a malignant dew. The frustration is so palpable you can scrape it off the walls. 'My heart is breaking,' wails Maya, as the radio announcer reads the morning news. 'We sit here calmly buttering toast while our jets are dropping bombs on Ishmalyia City. "You must not feel guilty," say the generals, "we only target military installations." But their soothing voices do not fool me. I see otherwise. I see women and children blown to pieces. I see undertakers remove ears from trees and fingers from the road. I see the bereaved. My brothers and my sisters. Have you forgotten, Zuni, that I too am bereaved?' I dispose of my toast and try to clasp Maya's hand, but it immediately takes flight as though my touch were poison. 'And what is my husband doing while all this is going on?' she asks mockingly. 'Why he spends every minute locked in his private world, where all the bodies are beautiful and every limb intact.'

Inca and Dr Hopi, back safely from the war zone, are immediately caught in the crossfire of our domestic strife.

'What shall I do?' I ask them in despair.

'Your wife has suffered a grievous loss,' says Dr Hopi.

'I haven't?' I say.

'Certainly,' says Dr Hopi, 'but Maya recognizes no parity in the distribution of pain. In her eyes you are untouched, essentially the same person. But she is not. Something was discharged from her body, which makes her less than she was. Generally she blames herself for this loss, hence the self-loathing and despair. But sometimes she blames you, hence her anger.'

'Me?' I say. 'Why me?'

'Perhaps she feels that you did not want the baby badly enough,' replies Dr Hopi.

'So all I have to do is convince my wife that I am not a heartless shit?' I conclude. Inca guffaws.

'I am not demanding the impossible,' says Dr Hopi, also smiling. 'In fact I advise you to do nothing. Just wait, wait for rationality to reassert itself over her more instinctive responses. It will before long, I promise you.'

'Well, that's solved that!' I say. 'Now tell me what I should do in the interim.'

'What should you do?' he cries. 'Why, work of course!'

'That's another problem,' I say.

'I have an alternative suggestion,' says Inca. 'Don't you think the time is ripe for us to bring out a special edition of *The Optimist?*'

'Inca,' I cry, 'you are a genius.'

Word is passed around the artistic community and we begin to receive contributions, among them a sheaf of iconoclastic poems from Cheyenne Zunz, spouse of *il Professore*. They are just up Maya's street.

> Summer and it is raining
> bombs,
> which bring forth
> strange unseasonal fruits.
> Blessed are the fruits of the earth,
> the arm as soft as a plum,
> the leg as fleshy as a melon,
> the head as complex as a pomegranate,
> and blood as red as a cherry.
> An early windfall,
> my summer harvest.

That sort of thing. The magazine is ready for distribution by October. It is a hot issue, full of fire and brimstone, in addition to poetry it contains letters from the front (letter bombs rather than belles-lettres), diaries of the campaign, and even some eyewitness accounts smuggled out of Ishmalyia City. I am not foolish enough to suppose that it will change anything, but it makes me feel better. Alas, the same cannot be said for Maya, who has come to resemble a yeti, both in appearance and smell. I comfort myself with the thought that things cannot get any worse. It is small comfort.

On a misty day in mid-October Maya cracks, or so it seems.

'I've had enough, Zuni,' she cries, 'please take me back to Dr Zecs.'

It is the moment I have been waiting for. 'I can do better than that,' I say, 'get washed and dressed and I'll introduce you to Professor Zunz himself. We'll go to his house tonight with a few advance copies of *The Optimist*.'

My wife is strangely compliant. She rises from the sofa and, an hour later, emerges from the bathroom bearing a distinct resemblance to her former self.

'Welcome back,' I say.

'Thank you,' she replies.

WE STEP INTO the Tatra and set off for the Valley of Figs, a semi-rural neighbourhood situated between the Mount of Olives and the Hill of Spies. In order to reach the Valley of Figs it is necessary to pass through the Old City. The quickest route to the Old City is by way of the leafy square which contains my memorial to the dead of '73. As we approach it appears to glow, apparently touched by St Elmo's fire. I regret to say that this is but a trick of the light, merely the verdigris shining beneath the silver moon. 'Now I know why she is weeping,' says Maya, examining her lachrymose doppelgänger through the windscreen; 'because she is a prophet, because she can see into the future.' Maya slumps back. 'But I was blind. I had no idea that I was posing for a monument to my own tragedy.'

'Our,' I say quietly, '*our* tragedy.'

'The possibility never occurred to me,' Maya continues, ignoring my interjection. 'Why should it? I was having fun. I enjoyed parading naked in front of you. I was proud of my body. I never gave a thought to the unfortunates who would come here when the thing was done. Well, I've been well and truly punished for my carelessness. I am one of them now.'

We enter the Old City through the Lion Gate and traverse its narrow lanes with headlamps dipped. It feels as though we are travelling along the backbone of Leviathan. The cobbles shine like fishy scales. The night air smells of cloves and roasting coffee. Several of the side-streets are little more than passageways. At their further ends men in white shrouds, made ghostly by the moonlight, sway in small groups, praying for the newly released souls of devout soldiers. The Old City is chock-a-block with believers. The secular and the wealthy tend to live in the valleys.

The house we seek is built of local limestone. Its walls are thick and the colour of honey, and it is surrounded by stands of *Ficus carica* in which countless *beccaficos* are roosting, like spirits in the body. I park my two-cylinder Tatra between a matching pair of de luxe Zorros and, offering my arm, escort Maya to the front door.

I am uncharacteristically optimistic. I feel like I am a figure in a fairy tale, knocking on the door of the wizard who will make good every ailment. It seems that our little drama is going to have a happy ending after all. I listen for the sound of approaching steps. Nothing, nada. Surely the deus ex machina is at home. I don't think I could bear a postponement now. 'Shall I knock again?' I ask. Maya shrugs. No need! The door suddenly opens. Professor Zunz himself stands within. Smiling I hold aloft a copy of the magazine and say, 'I thought your wife might like to see her poems in print.' No response. I look up at the Professor. It is obvious that he has not heard a word. In fact he is staring at me as though the sight of a human being were an entirely novel experience. True I am not expected, but surely my appearance cannot be that much of a surprise. The Professor's lips begin to move. I lean forwards endeavouring to catch the words. 'There has been a terrible tragedy,' he whispers.

My immediate inclination is to run. I grab Maya and prepare to flee from the Professor, and whatever it is that is eating his soul. But Zunz stops me in my tracks. He says, 'Come in.'

I smell a death, but whose? Have the authorities just telephoned with bad news about a son in the army? Has Mrs Zunz, the poet, suddenly expired? I glance in the dining room as we troop through the house, half expecting to see Cheyenne Zunz laid out on the table with sightless eyes and specs made of small change. Instead there is conventional silver cutlery, crested crockery, fluted glasses, and a crystal decanter full of red wine. Grief obviously arrived unexpectedly, nipping a dinner party in the bud. We cannot see the uninvited guest, but we can sense his presence, especially in the drawing room, where a small congregation sits dumbstruck.

Eyes closed, arms outstretched, the stricken hostess teeters centre stage, as though she were waltzing with grief in her sleep. Her face is white, as white as the masks the tragediennes wear at Epidaurus. In the background the kitchen door is ajar, sufficiently wide to reveal the main course; the hind leg of a spring lamb, swaddled in a shroud of sweet and sour linen. I can smell astringent effusions of vinegar, garlic, and juniper berries, and see charcoal still smouldering on the rotisserie. I picture Cheyenne Zunz, in happier circumstances, standing over the roasting gigot, occasionally basting the sizzling meat with red wine, olive oil, and its own dark juices. What can have happened in the last few minutes to abort this long-planned sacrifice?

You'll recall how the Almighty, wanting to test Abraham's loyalty, ordered him to slaughter his favourite son. Abraham bound the boy and was about to obey the commandment when, in the nick of time, a ram was caught in a thicket. Today, it appears, the roles have been reversed; the lamb escapes, the kid gets snuffed out. 'Last week our only son, whom we loved more than life itself, went with his school to the mountains,' explains the heartbroken Professor. 'We did not worry. Why should we? He was only sixteen, but he was already an experienced climber. Besides, he was with three teachers, all responsible fellows. Fat difference it made! When the avalanche came at midnight it swept away both the wise and the foolish, the prudent and the reckless. As it happens, all the party are accounted for. Save one. Our dear Tonto.'

'The irony is,' adds the anonymous academic on the sofa, 'that the avalanche was almost certainly caused by the pounding our boys are giving to Ishmalyia City. It seems that vibrations snaked along a fault line to the mountains.' He shakes his head. 'Can you believe it?'

The irony is lost on Maya. All she can see is another bereaved mother, a sister in distress, the personification of all those whose pain she had formerly shut out. Now is her opportunity to make amends. With a howl of anguish – both personal and for those others – she steps in on grief and clutches Cheyenne Zunz to herself. 'I know what you are feeling,' she cries between sobs, ending with an emphatic, '*I do know!*' Her words crash through the frozen sea that has encased Cheyenne Zunz and the two women are swept across the floor on a wave of unrestrained misery.

The Professor stares at the *danse macabre*. 'Your wife,' he says, 'is she all right?'

'Not exactly,' I say. 'She recently had a miscarriage. That's why we're here, really. I was hoping that you could reassure her, tell her what you're doing to defeat the genetic malfunction that has made her life a misery.' I grasp his forearm. 'What can I do, Professor Zunz? Except apologize for my bad timing. Another time, perhaps?'

'Yes,' he says, 'another time.'

'Please accept our condolences,' I say as I lead my bewildered wife to the door, pausing only to dump *The Optimist* in a magazine rack.

•

AS WE DRIVE home via the dark city — illuminated by nothing more than a single celestial bulb — all I can think about are the inherent agonies of parenthood. How unnumbered years of nurture, unnumbered years of unconditional love, can be undone in a moment, leaving behind nothing but heartache. What if it had been our child? What if he had survived the miscarriage, not to mention the possibility of cot-death, whooping cough, mumps, measles, meningitis, leukaemia, polio, cancer, kidnapping, sodomy, suicide, depression, automobile accidents, and other sundry dangers, only to be swept away in an instant by an avalanche of snow? Could we carry on? I look at Maya. Her eyes are puffy, her face pale. What are her thoughts? Evidently they are not the same as mine, because when we enter our house she says: 'Fuck me, Zuni. I want to make a baby.'

'I'll fuck you,' I reply, 'but not without a contraceptive. I don't think either of us could endure the trauma of another termination.'

But Maya will neither let the matter rest, nor let me be.

Later that night, when I am dozing in our double bed, she attempts to arouse me, hoping that I'll respond like Pavlov's dog and enter her before I realize what I'm doing. 'Insomnia,' I say, pushing her away, 'thy name is Maya.'

'Zuni,' she says, trying a different approach, 'when do you think Professor Zunz will make his breakthrough?'

'Soon,' I say, yawning.

Maya considers my response. 'Don't you think the search for his son's body may take the poor man's mind off his quest for a cure?' she says.

'I don't know,' I say. 'At first, perhaps, but when he

remembers that our future depends upon his efforts he'll not fail us.'

'It may be harder than he thinks,' she says. 'It may take years. I can't wait that long.' She muses. 'What would happen if we emigrated and had our baby overseas?'

'We would starve,' I reply. 'My career is here.'

'What about my life?' shouts Maya. 'Without a child it is meaningless, empty, unfulfilled.'

'You are young,' I say, 'there is plenty of time.'

'I want a baby now,' she says, 'before I change my mind, or my character. Who knows if I'll still be the same person come November?'

I try to make her see sense, but reason evidently has no influence over the biological imperative. Nor will I surren-der to desire. 'If we cannot have unconditional sex,' says Maya, finally proposing a truce, 'at least let's agree to confer with Dr Zecs.'

And so, twelve hours after our abortive visit to Professor Zunz, we are ushered into the chic consulting rooms of the celebrated obstetrician. On the wall is a burnished plaque with an English inscription: DR ZECS: SPECIALIST IN WOMEN & OTHER DISEASES. Yesterday morning Maya would have demanded absolution and oblivion of the doctor, but that was yesterday ... today she requires only permission to conceive. And Dr Zecs is clearly anxious to please. In the hospital Maya was nothing more than a damaged uterus with all the sexual allure of a squashed hedgehog, but now she is the magnetic north, the aurora borealis, and the good doctor cannot keep his eyes off her ... nor his hands. I can do nothing to stop him, of course, for society has granted him a

professional licence to probe at will. Subtract the qualifications and that plaque – a couple of letters and a slice of brass
– and what you have is a *cornuto* sitting in a room while,
barely hidden by a *cordon sanitaire*, a virtual stranger feasts
upon the privy parts of his wife. You may be thinking that
it's a bit late in the day for me to be worrying about my
wife's modesty, given that her charms are already on public
display, but when all is said and done a statue is no more
than a *corpus sine pectore*, a body without a soul, and all its
entrances and exits only culs-de-sac. Perhaps it is my imagination – my paranoia – but when Dr Zecs emerges from
behind the screen he appears to glow like a professional
gigolo. 'Maya tells me that she has mooted the possibility of
seeing out the pregnancy in another country,' he says, rolling
off the rubber gloves, newly glazed by my wife's juices. 'I
should like to make another suggestion; you stay where you
are, and let the mountain come to Mohammed.'

'What do you mean?' I ask.

'It so happens,' he says, 'that the religious authorities have
recently given their blessing to the importation of non-
Ashkenazi semen. Indeed, they consider it preferable to the
local product, since it greatly reduces the possibility of two
children of the same father falling in love and unwittingly trans-
gressing the prohibition on sexual relations between siblings.'

'What is the point?' I say.

'The point, my dear chap,' says Dr Zecs, 'is artificial
insemination.'

At least I can sleep unmolested. This seems to be the
only benefit of our visit to Dr Zecs. Maya has simply moved
from one extreme to the other; from lethargy to hyperactiv-

ity. She has taken it for granted that I will eventually give my blessing to the procedure, and is fizzing like seltzer. I try not to think about it, but in truth can think of little else. A few days ago I could not work, on account of the dead babies that haunted my imagination, now I am held back by living infants, the troublesome brood of other men.

Normally I disconnect the telephone when I am in my studio, but recently there has seemed little point in cutting myself off from the outside world. Let whole armies come from Porlock, there is no spell here for them to break. Most of the calls are well-meaning enquiries from Inca or Dr Hopi, but this is a voice I do not recognize.

'Now I know who you are,' it says gruffly, 'you're Zuni.'

'Correct,' I answer.

'This is Zunz,' it replies. 'Sorry about the other night. I was in such a state I don't think I'd have recognized my own mother. There's still no news, by the way. The silence is almost beyond endurance. Cheyenne calls me a monster because I flee to the laboratory every morning. She doesn't seem to appreciate that work alone keeps me sane. Take it away and I'd be worse than her. Poor Cheyenne is in a terrible state. Actually, that's why I'm phoning.'

'I'm a sculptor,' I say quickly, 'not a therapist.'

'Precisely,' says Zunz, 'and I want to commission you to assemble something in memory of Tonto. I don't know anything about art myself, so I'd like you to discuss the possibilities with my wife. If nothing else it'll occupy her mind, make her feel she's not completely helpless. What do you say?'

•

GRIEF AND STUPEFYING narcotics have turned Cheyenne Zunz into a zombie. As a matter of fact our ever-ingenious wholly indigenous pharmaceutical industry, stimulated by the state of permanent hostility, has developed and marketed a drug – pharaohzipan – specifically designed to deaden the ache consequent upon the loss of the first-born. But even that doesn't suffice for Cheyenne Zunz. 'When a dog is in unbearable pain they put it out of its misery,' she complains. 'I ask for no more.' By comparison Maya is comic relief. I offer the bereaved woman my arm and lead her through the Valley of Figs.

It is early and the morning dew still sits upon the lawns. Trees throw long shadows; some are beginning to turn, their leaves dusted with rouge like the cheeks of ageing courtesans. Hoopoes descend from the branches in undulating waves and pluck crickets from the grass. 'If I believed in reincarnation I'd swear that was Pocohontas returned to earth,' I say, as one of the promenading birds unfurls a prominent headdress of roseate feathers.

'Reincarnation,' mumbles Cheyenne Zunz, 'there's a thought.'

Goldfinches as cautious as cat-burglars pilfer brightly coloured berries from thick bushes, while wasps greedily devour the eponymous and overripe figs before spinning off drunkenly into the endless sky.

'Do you have any children?' asks Cheyenne Zunz.

'We were expecting a son,' I reply, 'but we lost him.'

'I see we have an experience in common,' says Cheyenne Zunz.

Tonto Zunz – missing, feared dead – was a star.

Academically gifted, musically attuned, good at all sports, especially basketball and soccer, popular with both sexes, yet not averse to his own company. Indeed he liked nothing better than to take the family dinghy on solo voyages across the inland sea, known appropriately as Lake Mono. Standing on the deck he would have squinted across the dazzling turquoise waters and seen, in the hazy distance, the snowy summit of Mount Nemo, little knowing that he was gazing upon the sublime figure of his assassin.

I picture him on that little yacht as I manipulate my alphabet of shapes. A dreamlike association of apparently unrelated objects – an anchor, a classical bust, and a wreath or arch of fig leaves – suddenly takes my fancy. On reflection I recognize that my unconscious has divined a hidden connection; all the articles speak of absence. The anchor implies a missing boat, the bust suggests an absent body, and the leaves are the souvenir of a tree, presumably from the Valley of Figs. I stand the disparate items on platforms – the woman facing the anchor, the wreath behind – in such a way as to suggest that an anchorless boat has sailed along the channel between them and beneath the bosky arch. Nor can the boat ever stop, since it no longer possesses its anchor. The anchor, I realize, is the key. It is the symbol of ancient seafarers, long departed. It represents memory; that which endures when all else has gone. It is something that functions in an alien element; iron in water, the past in the present. Finally, it echoes the ancient Egyptian symbol for life, coincidentally called the *ankh*.

The woman – who contemplates it – is loss incarnate (or

rather, disincarnate). The leaves are an opening to *pays inconnu*, from where no traveller returns. But it is not only the gateway to oblivion. Figs have a biblical (not to mention genital) association, so that the opening could also be that of the womb. Death thus becomes simultaneous rebirth. The whole being a defiant buoy in the River Lethe, a permanent reminder in the Valley of Figs. I cannot wait to show it to Cheyenne Zunz.

Has the pharaohzipan cast its spell, or has she sent it packing, deleted the analgesic from the prescription list? Either way Cheyenne Zunz is like a different person when I return to the Valley with my sketches. She examines them *con brio*, and declares herself well satisfied.

'Has there been some news?' I ask, astonished by the transformation.

'I'll say,' she replies.

It turns out that Cheyenne Zunz has been consulting a clairvoyant. 'I dare say you are sceptical,' she says. 'Men usually are. My husband certainly is. Don't fret, I won't hold it against you. Even I was dubious on my first visit. I don't know what I was expecting; perhaps a touch of mystery, a pinch of the supernatural, certainly crystal balls, chintz, and candlelight. Instead I find myself knocking at the door of Mrs Average. She lives in one of those terrible apartments they've put up to the north of the Old City. The interior confirms my worst prejudices. You know the sort of place; china ornaments on the shelves instead of books, plastic flowers on the television, and an anorexic Siamese on the settee. As for Mrs Seersucker herself, she is wearing a chrome-yellow housecoat, and her grey hair is set in a permanent wave. I am ready to make my excuses when she says, "I have a message for you, Mrs Zunz. From your son. He wants you to know that death is not the end."'

'She probably read about your loss in the papers,' I say.

'Exactly what my husband said,' she replies. 'And I would have to concede to you both if that were all. But she went on to tell me things about my family . . . intimate details . . . stuff only the inner circle knows. She is confident that she will be able to locate Tonto's body; what she calls "the redundant carapace of his wandering spirit". And I believe her. It's certainly true that I have become – as she promised I would – increasingly sensitive to my poor darling's presence in the house.' She picks up one of the sketches. 'That's why I've fallen in love with your idea,' she says, 'because it looks beyond death.' I agree to obtain estimates for the casting from the old-established Ashkenaz foundry of Anasazi & Son.

I make a small maquette, win the approval of the Professor, as well as his wife, and commence work upon the full-size sculpture. At least that is my intention. I step into my green overalls, mix the plaster, and start to construct a neo-classical bust. But I am subject to frequent interruptions as my wife, post-Zecs, buzzes in and out of my studio like a broody queen; the visitations being part of a continuous campaign, cunningly designed to force me to abdicate my procreative rights in favour of an anonymous other. Or so Maya maintains. In my opinion she secretly resents the time I am spending on the project, is jealous of my ability to lose myself in work. 'Is it my imagination,' she says, walking slowly around the bust, 'or are these the features of Cheyenne Zunz?'

'Of course not,' I reply, but on stepping back I see that she is absolutely right. Unconsciously I have reproduced my client's likeness. Sensing victory Maya presses home her advantage. 'It seems that it's acceptable to provide another woman – a virtual stranger, if you are to be believed – with a substitute for *her* son,' she says, overdosing on the sarcasm, 'but against the rules to give comparable comfort to your own wife.'

'Be reasonable, Maya,' I reply. 'The first is a statue, which may provoke various responses, but is essentially fixed; whereas the second is a journey without maps.'

'Zuni,' she snorts, 'you are a fraud. You claim to be redder than the Red Guards, but in reality you are a control freak. You cannot bear the idea of our son developing a will of his own.'

'That's not what worries me,' I reply. 'I'm frightened that he'll be the clone of a psychological defective or – worse still – a sociopath.'

'Why shouldn't he be a normal boy?' she asks. 'One who responds to nurture not nature.'

'No reason,' I reply, 'except that life has a built-in bias towards the unreasonable.'

'So why demand reasonableness of me?' asks Maya.

In general I do not work every day, but when the mood is on me and obstacles emerge, the frustration is worse than torture. So all Maya really has to do is persevere. Within the week, desperate to secure the solitude I require to complete the memorial, I surrender. I agree to all my wife's demands, and withdraw my objection to her being impregnated, in the near future, with the ejaculate of another man.

THE FOLLOWING MORNING Maya is back in my studio. 'What do you want now?' I snap.

'I thought this might be of interest,' she replies, handing me the *Ashkenaz Post*.

I look at the front page, which almost causes me to bring up my breakfast. It seems that our troops, still besieging Ishmalyia City, turned a blind eye while local desperados massacred the inhabitants of a nearby suburb. 'I always knew something like that would happen,' I say grimly.

'It's a terrible thing,' agrees Maya, 'but not why I brought you the paper. Turn the page.'

I do as instructed and immediately see a story headed: TONTO ZUNZ FOUND. For a ghastly moment I assume that he has been found alive, a fact which would — needless to say — make all my efforts redundant.

Then I read the text.

It tells how an expedition — consisting of a guide, a *Post* reporter, Cheyenne Zunz and the Professor — trekked to the summit of Mount Nemo and eventually discovered the boy's corpse at the bottom of an extinct fumarole. The guide led the way, of course. Having descended a narrow chimney they found themselves, so the journalist reported, at an open picture window built into a perpendicular wall, which looked out upon a celestial archipelago of swirling fog and alpine peaks. 'For one delirious moment,' the journalist wrote, 'we all knew what it was like to be one of the saved amid a multitude of the drowned, could sense how Noah felt when he surveyed the post-deluvian world from the safety of his buoyant ark.'

Nevertheless, the journalist continued, the place was empty; no relief, no sign of Tonto anywhere. Suddenly Cheyenne Zunz seemed to be overcome by some sibylline inspiration. Gravel dropped into the void as she stumbled to the very lip of the cave, forcing her companions to consider the possibility that she was contemplating a suicidal leap. No! She was leaning forwards, looking down, and screaming. Professor Zunz rushed to her side and, seeing what she had seen, clasped his face and cried out to his maker. The others did not need to be told what they had found. But, being curious, the journalist peered out and glimpsed, on the ledge below the cave, the body of Tonto Zunz preserved in ice. What was most note-worthy about the journey, however, was not the find itself, but the fact that it had been inspired by the dreamy vision of a clairvoyant. 'Every word is true,' confirms Cheyenne Zunz, 'Mrs Seersucker told us precisely where to look.'

THEY BURY TONTO on an autumnal morning in the ancient cemetery that covers a barren slope overlooking the Old City. Cheyenne Zunz clutches her husband's arm as four scruffy gravediggers slowly lower her boy into the hard ground. The Professor groans as the stiff corpse in its spotless shroud is swallowed like the snows of yesteryear. He looks like a man whose faith (if you can have *faith* in rationality) has been shaken to its foundations. As though having all his sentimental expectations dashed upon the rocks were not sorrow enough! Who knows what might happen next? If clairvoyants speak the truth, then anything is possible. Maybe he – Professor Zunz – could step into space and stroll upon the soft-bellied clouds as if they were *terra firma?* He stands beside the open grave, weeping for his poor boy, and for his former confidence in the material world. 'Zuni,' says Cheyenne Zunz, as we wander back towards our cars, 'forget the Valley of Figs, we have decided that this is the appropriate place for Tonto's memorial.'

The funeral seems to have pulled the plug on Maya's maternal instincts, or maybe she has cunningly switched tactics. Either way it has become possible for us to share breakfast without upsetting the marmalade. In fact we are mixing muesli and yogurt when the telephone rings.

Maya looks at the clock. 'It's very early,' she remarks.

'I'll get it,' I say. I lift the receiver.

'This is Dr Zecs' PA,' says a squeaky voice, 'calling to inform you that some suitable semen has unexpectedly become available. Can you come in right away?'

I gasp.

'Yes or no?' says the voice.

Maya is ecstatic, shot through with a joy that I cannot share. The rest of the morning proceeds like a dream. The hospital is overrun by boys from a local school queuing for their TB shots, so Dr Zecs is forced to find us a more private place. Maya undresses and sits open-legged on a chair in the middle of the room, as though she were an artist's model once again. The Doctor's face is glowing with admiration and desire, or so it seems to me. 'I must counsel your wife,' he says, bending at the waist and whispering in her ear. He squeezes her shoulder then retreats to his table where he pulls on articulated black gloves with tiny flash-lights at the fingertips. He picks up a highly polished silver syringe with numerous ducts at the tip. Maya spreads her legs as wide as they will go and Dr Zecs, his fingers illuminated, carefully inserts the needle into her vagina. The effort shows on his face. He is pushing hard. Suddenly the syringe is emptied into her and a many-branched fountain of silvery liquid emerges from between her thighs. I observe the procedure with growing discomfort. Maya, however, is radiant, like an expectant mother.

Now it is my turn to be counselled. 'Of course you appreciate,' says Dr Zecs, 'that Maya may still abort?' I nod. 'In which case,' continues the Doctor, 'would you prefer a day or night burial?'

'It makes no difference to me,' I reply indifferently.

The window of the room is open and a passing brass band drowns our words. Maya is upset by my lack of enthusiasm and rises to shut the window. She is still naked. 'You do realize that you – rather than the anonymous donor – may be the father of the foetus?' Dr Zecs remarks. In fact I hadn't considered the possibility. Dr Zecs hands me a book that has no words, only pictures. They illustrate mourners. All the mourners are children. Some are wearing sun-glasses. 'Those represent the night funerals,' Doctor Zecs explains. Why is he showing me this? I don't care, and I don't enquire. Maya gets dressed.

It begins to rain heavily. Nurse Lovic appears. She congratulates me and kisses Maya. She offers us an umbrella, only to discover that it has already stopped raining. We walk to the door. I am obviously sulking. 'We'll never know for certain,' says Maya, 'the child may be yours.'

'Not if it's a boy,' I reply. On the corner of the street some kids are restoring the rusty shell of a Tatra.

MAYA'S PREGNANCY is a paradigm. Every dawn she quietly rises from our bed. Then, having bowed to the sun, unrolls her yoga mat and performs a series of pre-natal exercises designed by a subcontinental swami. According to Nurse Lovic, Maya's midwife and guru, whom we see at regular intervals, these will tone up the dormant muscles required to project the unborn one into the world. 'You're perfect,' she says patting Maya's belly, which has begun to rise like yeasty dough, 'our little astronaut will pop out quicker than a champagne cork.' Maya continues with her gymnastics, adding some breathing exercises for good measure, confident that – this being a judicious universe – her conscientious preparations will bear fruit. Sure enough, nine months after the proxy impregnation, my wife gives birth to a healthy boy without breaking sweat. The news that a male-child has been safely delivered spreads rapidly and there is rejoicing throughout Ashkenazia; strangers slap my back or shake my hand, as if I had personally seeded the clouds and brought rain to a parched land. Taking the hint Inca titles his next column in the *Ashkenaz Post* THE DROUGHT IS OVER. At the naming ceremony I counterfeit enthusiasm, but secretly feel that I am appending my signature to another man's work.

Brimming with the milk of human kindness Maya suckles the foundling, while I seek sanctuary in the dragon's mouth.

Anasazi & Son is situated at the very edge of Ashkenaz, on a hill overlooking the eastern desert, a bone-dry wilderness of bleached rock. Forget the marital bed, forget the artist's studio, this is where the world begins, forged in the incandescent hearts of white-hot furnaces. Let there be light? Never! Heat is the alpha and the omega, the beginning and the end, and old man Anasazi is the true lord of creation, *mon dieu de la cire perdue*. He looks the part too, with his silver hair, his black eyes, his white beard, and his extraordinary fingers, which are both miraculously prehensile and microscopically precise. His voice is scorched and comes rumbling up from some internal echo chamber. If a volcano could speak it would sound like old man Anasazi.

'Congratulations,' he growls, pumping my arm. There is no escape. It seems that intelligence of my exceptional progeny has reached even here, the last outpost of civilization. I try to resemble a proud father, but feel like a back-street plagiarist pocketing unmerited praise.

'Where is your son?' I enquire, not finding his sweet face among the sweating minions.

'Where do you think?' he replies bitterly. 'In Ishmalyia, where else but Ishmalyia?'

He shakes his shaggy head, more prophet than divinity. 'Listen carefully, Zuni,' he says, fixing me with his mesmeric gaze. 'My only hope is that when the apple of your eye reaches the age of conscription our country will be at peace. For your sake, as well as his. I am far too old to fight, but am spared nothing; believe me, my friend, I am going through hell. I would not wish such worry on my worst enemy. It isn't enough that I have to lie abed terrified lest my boy falls in battle, now I also have to pray that he doesn't commit some unforgivable atrocity.' He mops his brow with a soiled rag. 'Don't get me wrong,' he says, 'he is a beautiful lad, but he was raised on paradox, is used to watching great works of art emerge – Abednego-like – out of the fiery furnace, and so may just fall for the nonsense that a new order will spring from the inferno. He may just be persuaded that destruction is a necessary prelude to creation, that the Ishmalites are as ephemeral as wax in the kiln.'

Personally I see the wax in more abstract terms, as an idea, a premonition, that which gets lost in translation. Classical deities utilized petrification as a punishment, which may explain why I get this feeling of delinquency every time I sign a contract with old man Anasazi, why I sense that I am betraying my inventions, limiting their infinite possibilities to one. But what choice do I have? Wax will soften under the unremitting Ashkenazi sun as surely as the wings of Icarus. For a memory – I mean, memorial – to be lasting it must be cast in bronze. And so, while Maya remains at home posing bare-breasted as the Madonna *de nos jours*, I slip out of the house like a Dadaist burglar with my enigmatic booty, an anchor, a bust, and a wreath of fig leaves. Moulds of the originals are made at the foundry, from which the wax replicas are eventually obtained. (Herein lies old man Anasazi's special genius, with his preternatural fingers he can exactly reproduce the minutest detail of the kernels in the clones.) These, in turn, are covered with a heat-resistant compound and slowly baked in a brick oven until the wax is lost, whereupon the empty moulds, vacated by the understudies, are transferred to a pit and filled with molten bronze. I always like to be present when old man Anasazi, swaggering like some hellish obstetrician, plucks my baby from its smouldering womb with tongs of iron. 'Perfect,' he wheezes, cracking open the mould with a single hammer-blow.

Tonto Zunz's memorial is duly erected. In time it sprouts a green patina, as if it were a growing thing, an elaborate nettle, drawing sustenance from the salts and gases released by the decomposing corpse beneath. It becomes, I am pleased to note, a place of pilgrimage. 'It is like a magnet,' says my satisfied client, 'that draws forth my memories.' Maya, too, turns out to be a dedicated mother. Thanks to her selfless ministrations the baby develops with startling precocity; it sits, gives its first smile, masters crawling, eats its first solids, stands, and – long before the end of its first year – takes its first steps and learns to say 'mama' and – to my discomfort – 'dada'. Fortunately Maya is so overwhelmed by maternity, so absorbed in her son's resourcefulness, that she fails to register my indifference. Far from it!

THE INVASION OF Ishmalyia is well into its third year. As the casualties mount its unpopularity increases. There are daily demonstrations outside the Prime Minister's office. Right-wing politicians talk ominously of betrayal, accuse the dissidents of stabbing the army in the back. Mothers, save Maya, are still refusing to breed boys. Nor is the Professor any nearer finding a cure for what is now known as the Zunz Syndrome. Our prodigal child sleeps in its cot. We are sitting on the sofa, watching recent developments on the late-night news. 'I feel so guilty,' says Maya.

'Why?' I ask.

'Because I am so happy,' she replies. 'We live in such terrible times, yet I am happier than I have ever been before. Tell me, Zuni, am I a wicked person?'

'Of course not,' I say, kissing her.

'Thank you Zuni,' she says.

'Now it is my turn to feel guilty.'

'Let's tempt fate,' she says suddenly, 'let's take a risk, let's make a baby of our own. I want us to make love unprotected. I want us to be vulnerable, unskinned, as naked as bananas, as intimate as two people possibly can be.' I have no desire to hurt her, besides I am bemused, bedazzled, beguiled and seduced. I am also impatient. 'Wait, my love,' whispers Maya, 'let me prepare myself. I want to give you a night to remember.' She does. I'll never forget that Wednesday, that 6th of July.

SHE WALKS TOWARDS the bathroom. At the door she turns and blows a kiss. I hear the water running, then the radio as she relaxes in the steaming, fragrant water. The radio is playing popular music, torch songs and ballads sung by husky-voiced sirens. I smile. Maya must have retuned it before disrobing, turned the dial away from the baleful round-the-clock news service she tends to favour. Buildings, like radio stations, also have a unique frequency, which determines how they vibrate during the course of an earthquake. When the frequency coincides with the speed of the quake the two forces combine like lovers in unison. The intensity can be devastating. It has a name, it is called resonance. Resonance acts like a loud-speaker, it amplifies

162

the effect. If our house were not properly designed, like all properties outside the Old City, to roll with the punches, to sway with the flow of the seismic waves, the resonance would probably have demolished it thirty seconds ago. At first I do not think *earthquake*. My initial assumption is that the Ishmalites are bombarding the city, but this is easily dismissed, the sound effects are wrong; no explosions, nor echoing thumps, just creaking and cracking, as though sinews and bones were being stretched and snapped.

The phone rings. It sounds like a chainsaw slicing through air. Only then does it register that the house is otherwise completely silent. I answer the phone. It is Inca. 'Are you all OK?' he asks. Why isn't the radio still working?

'Hold on a minute,' I say. I trot towards the bathroom. The door is open. I enter. The boy is within, staring into the tub. 'Get out!' I shout. He doesn't budge. 'Fuck off! Fuck off, you little bastard!' I scream, raising my arm. The boy runs away, whimpering like a banished puppy. I see what I see. I see the radio in the water. I see Maya under the water. I see blue lips, I see pupils so dilated that the irises are black. Maya looks exactly what she is, someone who has died of shock. Of course I should unplug the radio, pull out the little death's head that connects it to the mains, I should unplug the drain, let out the water. Who knows, perhaps a spark of life lingers behind that insensate stare? But I do nothing. I choose not to rupture the transparent membrane that has formed above the corpse, I want it preserved, fossilized in water. I try to concentrate on the beauty of the object within, the concupiscent woman awaiting her lover, but I can hear the kid still blubbing somewhere in the house. 'Go to your room!' I cry. Fearful, he obeys.

I return to the bathroom with pastels and paper. Now I can think, can respond properly to the tragedy. I start to draw Maya. In a way her last wish has come true. She is certainly open to the world, completely open, infinitely vulnerable, her body no longer her own. My hand moves automatically as I capture the face, itself displayed like a portrait under glass. I pause only to consider which blue to use for the lips, rejecting lapis lazuli, and aquamarine, as well as sapphire, cobalt, and cerulean, all too gaudy, too reminiscent of summer skies, before settling upon dismal, banal Prussian blue. Maya's upper lip is slightly curled, revealing her perfect teeth. Descending I crown my beauty's breasts with pink puckered coronets, and am tempted to decorate the dark weedlike fronds that sway between her legs with tiny silverfish. But when I am done I look upon the picture with despair. Maya just isn't there, she has metamorphosed into nothing, has vanished into thin air. Whatever she was thinking about on the cusp between life and death has died with her. The authorities are welcome to this inanimate impostor. I walk to the telephone and am surprised to find the receiver already dangling from its side. I pick it up. 'Anyone there?' I say.

'You certainly know how to build up the suspense,' replies Inca.

'It is Maya,' I say, 'she's dead.'

GLOVED HANDS plunge through the meniscus and drag my limp, unprotesting wife dripping from the matrix. Later, with my permission, surgeons open her up and remove her vital organs for transplantation. They also cut out her eyes, intending to use the corneas. Finally the eclipsed, eviscerated cadaver is burned at the local crematorium. I stand in the front row with the boy, both of us clutching roses, while behind the scenes an underling watches the holocaust through a peephole. The coffin burns first, after which my wife is consumed by fire. The process takes ninety minutes. Nothing comes out save ashes. *Ma femme est perdue*, my wife is lost.

The pharaohzipan doesn't work. Nor are counsellors any help. Neither can raise the dead. Not that I consider Maya among the dead: she was too young, too beautiful, too full of plans. Even so her absence is undeniable and – to tell the truth – I can explain it no other way. Actually, I can accept that she died. To die is to change from one state to another; it is an active verb, implying the possibility of further alterations, but to be dead *au contraire* is to be eternally passive, permanently excluded. It is not in character, not Maya's style. And so I am almost prepared to believe Cheyenne Zunz when she shows up with a communication from Mrs Seersucker.

'I don't want to cause you any distress,' she says, 'but there's something I've been meaning to tell you for ages. It's taken me this long to pluck up the courage.'

'Go ahead,' I say.

'Well, I happened to visit my clairvoyant a few days after the earthquake. I don't know why, I suppose I needed reassurance. Anyway, before I can utter a word she says, "Does the name Zuni mean anything to you?" I'm flabbergasted needless to say, and tell her that a friend of mine – named Zuni – has just lost his wife. "In that case," she says,

"I've got some good news for him. His wife has contacted me from the other side. When I saw her she was dancing. She was born to dance, or so she said. She asked me to let her family know that she was very happy. She was surrounded by blue, lots of soft blue fabrics. And shoes. She was very proud of all her shoes." What do you think?'

'I'm glad you told me,' I say, 'but I don't know. I find it hard to imagine the *champs-élysées* lined with shoe shops.'

Although I find it difficult to picture Maya as a foot fetishist in the next world, at least I have irrefutable evidence that she was once an inhabitant of the here and now. Feeling uncomfortably like a necrophiliac I haunt the square where her statue resides (and now weeps for its missing twin), I pour over my intimate sketches. I even resort to a magnifying glass to confirm the memory of her hidden beauty. But nothing is as potent a mnemonic as the boy who daily grows more like her. I experience déjà-vu every time I glimpse his face, and yet I cannot love him; try as I might I cannot bring myself to love my wife's living memorial. Dr Hopi scours his textbooks on my behalf but can find no explanation for this failure, save the obvious. No, it is more than the fact that I am not his biological father. He is handsome, like his mother, but he is strange like no one else. I am an artist and am, by definition, self-centred and selfish. But I am a communist compared to the boy, who has yet to outgrow his infantile need for instant gratification. His desires and his actions are as well coordinated as synchronized swimmers.

•

I GET AN IDEA. 'Hey,' I say, 'let's go to Moho for a treat.' This may sound perverse, but I want him to like me, even if I can't warm to him, if only for Maya's sake. We travel along the familiar road to the coast. The boy is sullen throughout the journey, seemingly preoccupied. Upon arrival he takes one look at the sea – which, admittedly, is somewhat tempestuous – and turns screaming from the sight. When I prepare to dive in he becomes hysterical; more, deranged. I am compelled to drive him home the same day. Dr Hopi almost shakes me when I report the incident. 'How insensitive can you get?' he cries accusingly. 'The boy was obviously traumatized by finding his mother dead in the bath. So how else do you expect him to react when he is confronted with such a vast expanse of water? It obviously brought back the entire experience. You should be ashamed of yourself, Zuni, for exposing him to such an ordeal.'

CHEYENNE ZUNZ becomes a frequent visitor, almost a regular fixture. I assume initially that she is proselytizing on behalf of Mrs Seersucker, is intent on persuading me that the woman has become Maya's *poste restante* on earth. But it soon becomes clear that this is merely a smokescreen, that her real agenda is otherwise. But what is it? Does she have designs upon me? Is the Professor too absorbed in his own work to notice her? Does he fail to satisfy her carnal needs? She is certainly a fine-looking woman, with chestnut hair and a voluptuous figure which she makes no great effort to conceal. For example, when she leans toward me to vouch-safe the latest spiritual communiqué from the clairvoyant – lest the boy overhears – fleshier secrets are inevitably revealed. Are these the wiles of a practised seductress, or the innocent gestures of a happily married woman who has long since forgotten the universal power of her charms? Or is my vanity causing me to bark up the wrong tree? Perhaps the visits have nothing to do with me at all. It is certainly true that Cheyenne Zunz spends as much time on her knees with the boy as she does talking to me, smothering him with hugs and kisses. At this rate it won't be long before he starts calling her 'mama'. Is this why she comes? Because she regards him as a substitute for Tonto, a motherless child for a childless mother? The more I consider this possibility the more likely it seems. Then it occurs to me that Cheyenne Zunz may be privy to something that I am not. And so the next time she shows up with another infantile novelty I put on my jacket, announce that I have a important meeting to attend, and unceremoniously ask her to look after the boy.

'Do you have an appointment with Dr Zecs?' asks the secretary. 'That won't be necessary,' I reply, pushing past her and entering the obstetrician's plush consulting rooms. Dr Zecs is sitting at his mahogany desk manicuring his fingernails.

'Zuni!' he cries, lazily looking up. 'This is a pleasant surprise. I was very sorry to hear about Maya . . . needless to say. Tell me, how are things with you and the boy? He is in good health, I trust.'

'We are both as well as can be expected,' I reply.

'Good, good,' he says, clicking the scissors. He looks at his watch. 'Is there anything I can do for you?' he asks cautiously.

'As a matter of fact there is,' I reply, 'I need to know the identity of the boy's father.'

'Zuni,' he says, smiling and open-handed, showing me his perfect teeth and his perfect cuticles, 'you must know that such information is confidential. And even if it weren't I couldn't tell you because I don't know.'

'So where did the semen come from in the first place?' I ask.

'I can't tell you that either,' he replies.

I may not be a member of the working class but my hands are strong and calloused. I lean across the desk and place them around the doctor's throat, slowly constricting his windpipe.

'You're a maniac,' he gasps.

I continue to confirm the diagnosis.

'Enough!' he hisses. 'I'll tell you. The semen was supplied by Professor Zunz.'

As if I hadn't guessed!

I find the Professor in his laboratory at the University of Ashkenaz's medical school. He is wearing a white coat, plastic goggles, and is holding a test tube boiling over with unknown gases. He looks the part. 'Hello, Zuni,' he says, 'what are you doing here? I thought you were with Cheyenne.'

'She's at my house,' I reply, 'playing with her grandson.'

'Her *what*?' he gasps.

'You heard,' I say. 'The imposture is at an end. I have discovered your secret. I don't know how you did it but somehow you salvaged the sperm from Tonto and arranged for Zecs to inject it into Maya. Scientists are expected to be cold-hearted, but you are a monster, Zunz. You used an innocent woman as your son's surrogate wife. Now it's time to acknowledge the truth and adopt the unfortunate off-spring as your own.'

'You are deluded, my friend,' says the Professor, shaking his head, 'grief has obviously deranged you.'

'There's no mistake,' I reply, 'you only have to see Cheyenne with him to know.'

'Think, man!' yells Professor Zunz. 'How can Tonto be the father? He was an Ashkenazi. Your boy is a boy. If Tonto had been the father there would have been a miscarriage in the fourth month.'

'Not necessarily,' I reply, 'the whole world knows that you are a genius, a master of genetic engineering, you could have done what was required right here.'

'And you are a madman,' he says, 'I could no more do what you suggest than you could bring your wife's statue back to life.'

'You're lying,' I say, 'if you refuse to tell me the truth I'll have to go elsewhere, to your wife for example.'

The Professor puts down the test tube, removes his goggles, and sighs. 'My dear Zuni,' he says, looking me in the eye, 'there is, I'm afraid, a fatal flaw in your argument. The body we found in the ice wasn't Tonto's.

'I don't believe you,' I say.

'I didn't think you would,' he says wearily. 'Fortunately the proof is right here, in this very building. Follow me and you shall see it for yourself.' He leads me along artificially lit corri-dors that seem more suited to a fairground or a freak show than to a scientific institution; there are cages full of mutant mice and jars crammed with a variety of nature's other mistakes.

'As a matter of interest,' I say, 'if it wasn't Tonto's, then whose funeral did we attend?'

'There is no shortage of bodies at present in Ashkenazia,' Professor Zunz replies, 'I simply borrowed an unclaimed one from the morgue.'

'Does Cheyenne know?' I ask, wondering if she too was acting on that bittersweet day.

'Of course not,' he snaps. 'You have touched upon my greatest dread, that someday she will see through the deception, will realize that the final resting place of our son remains unknown, his body unburied. I fear her sanity will not survive the shock.'

We reach a pair of swing doors with inset portholes. 'Look inside,' says my guide. 'That's what we brought down from the mountain.'

I peer into a twilight world which possesses but a single inhabitant, a solitary man, eternally slumbering on a stone lilo at the bottom of an empty swimming pool. 'I grant you he's dead,' I say, 'but why should I take your word that you found him on Mount Nemo?'

'Where else could he have come from?' replies the Professor impatiently. 'The man is unique. For a start, he is over five thousand years old.'

'Are you seriously expecting me to accept that you mistook an emaciated relic from the Neolithic era for your own son?' I enquire, more incredulous than ever.

'We all did,' replies the Professor calmly. 'As you can see the Iceman's left arm – we call him the Iceman – has been flung protectively across his face as if trying to disguise his features (or, more likely, to ward off life's final blow). But that barely suffices as an explanation, let alone an exculpation. In fact there are no excuses. Our expectations were such that it simply didn't occur to any of us that we had come upon someone other than Tonto. In short, my friend, we experienced a collective hallucination.'

The swing doors squeakily part and Zunz summons me into the cold and crepuscular room. I shiver, not because of the chill, but because of fear. I feel as though I am in the presence of some ancient mischief-maker whose power to deprave remains menacingly potent. Professor Zunz observes my reaction. 'Interesting,' he murmurs, 'you sense it too.'

FIAT LUX. Zunz touches the switch and electric light erratically enters the dead world. We stand like gods at the dawn of creation watching the clay begin to twitch with life. Could the Iceman really be stirring? Of course not! The flickering neon strips have created a strobelike effect which, in turn, has produced the illusion of movement. Within moments the light is bright and constant, and the Iceman once more in the frosty grip of rigor mortis. 'It is a tremendous find,' says the Professor. 'Not only do we have this chap's body in a perfect state of preservation, but we also have his clothes and his weapons, which is why we can date it so confidently.' He beckons me to the dead man's side. 'Consider his flesh,' he continues enthusiastically. 'It ought to be horrible and greasy, the technical term is adipocere, but waxlike will suffice. However, thanks to some inexplicable fluke, it's still pretty fresh. The lucky fellow must have been freeze-dried and frozen within seconds of death. Nor were his remains picked over by foxes or bears, as you would expect. Indeed, if it weren't for Mrs Seersucker's faulty vision he would certainly have continued undisturbed until Doomsday.'

'When did you realize that Mrs Seersucker was a fraud, that you hadn't found Tonto?' I ask.

'Not on the mountain,' replies the professor, 'our mistake only became apparent when we got back to the lab and lifted the body from its sepulchre of ice.'

'Why didn't you tell Cheyenne at once?' I ask.

'Of course I meant to,' replies the Professor, 'but I didn't know how. I couldn't find the words. Then she announced that we had found Tonto and it was already too late. *Iacta est alea*, the die was cast.'

There is but one thing left to ask. 'OK,' I say, if it wasn't Tonto's semen then whose was it?'

Professor Zunz points to the Iceman. 'Behold,' he says, 'the father of your son.'

I examine the freeze-dried stiff. 'Not only are you crazy,' I say, 'you're also sick.'

'Be that as it may,' he replies, 'but the fact remains that when I opened up the cadaver I discovered that there was still life in the old dog, which is to say that there was viscous semen in the cord connecting the testes to the penis. But was it viable, did it possess vitality? I decided to risk an experiment. I gave it to Zecs.'

I do not hit him. Nor do I slaughter the kid. After all he is half Maya's.

•

ONCE I WANTED to conquer the world with my art, confidently expected to join the immortals. Now my ambitions are more modest. I am Zuni the stonemason, Zuni the memorial-maker. At present I am cutting into the bole of an ancient oak. I can see Maya's body within it as clearly as I saw her corpse in the bath but, far from being an aide mémoire, the emerging woman only serves to remind me how much I have already forgotten. I am a competent craftsman, well able to portray her beauty, but with every blow I strike I inevitably betray her quicksilver spirit and my art. It is beyond my talent to recreate the texture of her skin, the taste of her kisses, the manifold scents of her sweats and emissions, the sweet sound of her voice, the throb of her inner life. I have no power to oxygenate the wood, or pump hydrogen through its pores. I can reconstruct the vessel, but the contents ... the contents are spilled and evaporated. *Ma femme est perdue.* Maya is lost, and I shall soon be forgotten. When I am gone only the memorials I have built as a solace for others will remain, and my son, who grows more beautiful and more debauched by the day.

In Praise of Impurity

THE GREAT HALL of the Palace of Culture is packed to hear Professor Zunz address the Ashkenazian Association for the Advancement of Science on the vexed subject of future generations. The main speaker fidgets as he is introduced, making his apprehension apparent to all. He had never intended to make his most radical experiment public, but rumours in the press, orchestrated by a cynical hack named Inca, have left him with little choice. He rises, smiles sadly at the front row, which contains Cheyenne, his own bereaved wife, and then candidly admits to initial failure; despite having isolated and carefully studied the rogue gene that is unmanning their nation, he is still unable to disarm it. He lifts his hands to quell the utterances of disappointment and despair his *mea culpa* has occasioned. 'Did I give in? Did I accept defeat?' he asks rhetorically. 'I did not! I simply took a different route to the solution.' Now his smile is triumphant, rather than melancholy.

'To cut a long story short,' he continues, 'I proceeded by analogy. I considered the behaviour of the humblest of metals. Even when placed in sulphuric acid pure zinc stays incorruptible, immunized by its purity. Only when impurities are added will it react. There was obviously a wider lesson to be drawn from this example, as my esteemed colleague, Primo Levi, makes clear in his invaluable study, *The Periodic Table*. I quote. "One could draw from this [that is, the behaviour of pure zinc] two conflicting philosophical conclusions: the praise of purity, which protects from evil like a coat of mail; the praise of impurity, which gives rise to changes, in other words, to life. I discarded the first, disgustingly moralistic, and I lingered to consider the second, which I found more congenial. In order for the wheel to turn, for life to be lived, impurities are needed, and the impurities of impurities in the soil, too, as is known, if it is to be fertile. Dissension, diversity, the grain of salt and mustard are needed: Fascism does not want them, forbids them, and that's why you're not a Fascist; it wants everybody to be the same, and you are not. But immaculate virtue does not exist either, or if it exists it is detestable."'

Professor Zunz takes a deep breath. 'Well,' he confesses, 'I have added an impurity to Ashkenazia's pristine genetic pool,' carefully including the magic formula, 'with the permission of our foremost religious authorities.' He then proceeds to tell his astonished audience about the strange nativity of Zuni's son, sparing no details, not even the identity of the incredible sperm donor, still known only as the Iceman.

'How can you be sure that Maya's husband was not the father, or even someone else?' demands a sceptical listener. 'She was not exactly the Virgin Mary.'

'Believe me,' replies Zunz, 'there is no doubt as to the paternity. The child is male. Therefore his father cannot be an Ashkenazim. That is our problem, our curse. Besides, you only have to look at the boy to recognize that he is not one of us.'

'If he is not one of ours,' comes the obvious rejoinder, 'to whom does he belong?'

'A fair question,' replies Zunz, 'I only wish I could provide a definitive answer. But the truth is that our saviour's pedigree remains a mystery. In his case there are no certainties, only speculations. The fact that we discovered the Iceman on the slopes of Mount Nemo, near the body of my poor son, and that his flesh had not been devoured by wild beasts was obviously of some significance, but I did not put two and two together until I recalled the title of another of Primo Levi's books, that is *The Drowned and the Saved*. What I am going to suggest may sound far-fetched, but I began to contemplate the possibility that Iceman had been a victim – or even a survivor – of Noah's Flood. Why not? His post-glacial potency was already a miracle. Anyway, a scientist should exclude no explanation, however outlandish. This interpretation would certainly account for his recourse to higher ground, and the absence of predators. I am no expert in such matters, so I turned to our holy texts for guidance, as well as Louis Ginzberg's *The Legends of the Ashkenazim*. The latter being particularly suggestive.'

Acknowledging it as his chief source he offers the following scenario which is, he emphasizes, nothing more than a theoretical possibility.

'THE STORY GOES that at the time of the deluge the world was a divided between the descendants of Cain,' continues Professor Zunz, warming to his task, 'and the descendants of Seth. Whereas the former resembled their forefather in sinfulness and depravity, the latter led blameless, well-regulated lives. If anything their existence was too well regulated, too comfortable: a single sowing bore a harvest sufficient for the needs of forty years; pregnancy lasted but days, giving rise to a progeny so precocious that they were born walking and talking and well able to sever their own umbilical cords. Alas the devil soon found work for such curious and idle hands.

'Before long the descendants of Cain and the descendants of Seth were indistinguishable in their iniquities. In time the latter even forgot their jealous benefactor. Needless to say, he didn't forget them.

'Two angels, Azazel and Shemhazai, the Rosencrantz and Guildenstern of the divine court, observed the distress caused to their master by the idolatrous practices carried on by his favourites below, and volunteered to descend and remind the children of Seth of their obligations. "O Lord of the world!" they cried. "It has happened, that which we foretold at the creation of the world and of man, saying, 'What is man, that thou art mindful of him?'"

'"And what will become of the world now without man?" God replied.

'"We will occupy ourselves with it," said the angels.

'"I am well aware of it," replied God, "and I also know that if you inhabit the earth, the evil inclination will overpower you, and you will be more iniquitous than ever men were."

'"Grant us but permission to dwell among men," pleaded the angels, "and thou shalt see how we sanctify thy name."

'Ever susceptible to flattery the king of kings yielded to their wishes. "Descend," he thundered, "and sojourn among men!"

'The inevitable occurred. First Azazel and Shemhazai fell to earth, then they fell from grace. Their heads were turned by the daughters of Cain, who habitually went about their business in a state of *déshabillé*, and the daughters of Seth, who were only marginally more modest. As well as being shameless both were given to bestial practices and every conceivable manner of lewd appetites, which they satisfied whenever the fancy took them. Of such were the women, whose beauty and sensual charms tempted the angels from the path of virtue.

'The earthbound duo quickly lost their transcendental qualities, and duly gained the ability to mate with the voluptuous aborigines. Their numerous offspring were known variously as *emim*, because they inspired fear, *rephaim*, because one glance at them made the heart grow weak, *zamzummim*, because they were masters of war, and *nephilim*, because, by bringing the world to its fall, they themselves fell.

'Even among the *nephilim* the youngest child of Azazel and Naamah was unusually precocious. By the age of sixteen he had assimilated the entire sum of human knowledge, such as it was; he knew the names of all the flora and fauna, and of the stars in the firmament. He knew how to sow, and reap, and cook meat. He knew the way of a man with a maid. In fact he already knew several ways of a man with a maid. He knew too much, and not enough.

'One day he quit his birthplace and strode ever westward

across the hills in the direction of Eden, determined to eat of the forbidden tree. The sky as ever was primary blue, save for one small quadrant, which was as purple as a bruise. Forked lightning flickered from its hollow centre, as though it were a nest of phosphorescent vipers. The occasional flashes illuminated a natural amphitheatre, which was filled with unearthly creatures in dark uniforms. Some held flaming brands, while others carried banners which were surmounted with brazen rocs. At their head, elevated by a dais, was the figure of a man whose corpus was made not of flesh but of fire. He too wore a uniform, which smouldered, but was not consumed. Across his chest were rows and rows of medals, more numerous than those that adorned the breast of Mars. His voice was louder than Thor's, but surprisingly shrill. Every time he paused bands of angels blew trumpets. The curious *nephilyte* concealed himself in a bunker and observed the ceremony. He did not like what he heard.

'"Is it not true that the *nephilim* have rebelled against me saying, 'There is no God!'? ranted the great creator. "Have I not been patient with them these hundred and twenty years? I have stayed my hand, and they have turned their backs. They have poisoned the earth, so that everything that steps upon it is corrupted, even my angels. If their only crimes were blasphemy, curiosity, mischief, and unholy laughter, I might yet have spared them, but they are rapacious too. When a farmer brings a basket of fruit to market, they will edge up to it, one after another, and each steal a bit, until the farmer has nothing left to sell. If he has nothing to sell, there will be no profit, and without profit there will be no effort. I offered order, both moral and economic, but even my best beloved have opted for anarchy instead. Very well, let them learn the true meaning of anarchy. I shall bring ruin upon the earth, annihilate its inhabitants, wipe every trace of them from the face of the earth. All I need do is lift my restraining hand from the elements, and allow the world to revert to its original state of eternal chaos. Then let them repent their folly and their misdeeds. Then let them know the anger of their maker. But to remove only the cancerous cells will not suffice, mankind itself has been infected beyond repair by the example of the *nephilim*, and has placed itself beyond redemption. It too must be erased, so that new generations will cleave to my commandments, and remain pure in body and in heart."

'Then the *nephilyte* listened as Uriel was called forth and sent to Noah. Uriel was told to reveal that the Lord intended to do a new thing in the earth, to visit a great destruction upon it, to wit a deluge for one year, when all creatures that are on the earth shall die, save for Noah and his family. "And there will be a great punishment on the earth," continued the creator, "and the flood will cleanse the earth of all impurity." Finally Uriel was ordered to teach Noah how to construct an ark from gopher wood. Next Raphael was instructed to put the fallen angel Azazel into chains, cast him into a pit of sharp and pointed stones in the desert Dudael, and cover him with darkness, where he was to remain until the Day of Judgement, when he would be thrown into the fiery pit of hell, and the earth would be healed of the corruption he had brought to it. Shemhazai was to be suspended between heaven and earth, in the position of a penitent sinner. Gabriel was charged to act against the bastards and reprobates, the sons of the angels conceived with the daughters of Cain and of Seth, that is to say, the *nephilim*. The angels cheered, saluted their leader, and proceeded to follow his perscription to the letter.

'The horrified *nephilyte* abandoned his journey and returned to warn his father, Azazel, and his mother, Naamah, and all his brothers and sisters, of the fate that awaited them. "We are all to be destroyed for the sin of stealing apples," he announced. They thought he was joking and paid no heed, even when the sun was darkened and the rains gathered in the altostratus. "If the waters of the flood come from above, they will never reach up to our necks," they boasted, "and if they come from below, the soles of our feet are large enough to dam up the springs." Heedlessly they continued to lead unchaste lives and to rob the farmers of their fruits. Even after the rains began.

'After forty days and nights they stopped laughing. In the end some even sought to delay their death agonies by casting their own children into the springs, in a vain attempt to choke the waters that issued from below. But they could do nothing to quench the unstoppable torrents that poured upon them from the heavens, for the long arm of God had plucked two stars out of the constellation Pleiades. More-over, each drop of the never-ending rain passed through Gehenna before it fell to earth in the form of boiling water. As their sensual desires had made them hot, so were the *nephilim* chastized, though some might consider being boiled alive an excessive punishment for sexual abandon and shoplifting.

'It was a sort of global chemotherapy, so to speak, knocking out the good and the bad indiscriminately.

'Of all the *nephilim* who lived at the time of the flood only one still breathed when Noah's over-laden ark began to float upon the surface of the waters. The last of the *nephilim*, whose warnings had been mocked and ignored, first begged Noah to take him on board, as he had accommodated Og, the giant King of Bashan; then, having failed in that, he swam to the side of Mount Nemo, which he commenced to climb. As he ascended he noticed that the rain ceased to scald his skin, indeed it became pleasantly cool. This was just as well, for he could not rest. As fast as he climbed, the waters rose faster. And then the rain ceased, or rather it changed form. It was now soft and white, and so cold that the *nephilyte*, for all his exertions, began to shiver. The flood water also altered, and became a hard, glassy substance. Whatever the cause it ceased to rise. Feeling safe at last the *nephilyte* rested upon a ledge. Sleep overcame him, snow covered him. During the night his body froze, but the seed within him did not die.'